BUILD

UNIVERS

Anabel Altenburg

A Sculpted World

© 2022 **Europe Books**| London

www.europebooks.co.uk | info@europebooks.co.uk

ISBN 9791220119801

First edition: March 2022

Distribution for the United Kingdom:
Vine House Distribution Ltd

Printed for Italy by *Rotomail Italia S.p.A. - Vignate (MI)*
Stampato presso *Rotomail Italia S.p.A. - Vignate (MI)*

A Sculpted World

To my parents, whom I love with my whole heart.

Man is above all else mind, consciousness – that is, he is a product of history, not of nature.

Antonio Gramsci

Chapter One

I lie wrapped up in a set of stripy cotton pyjamas, my head in a cloud of pillows and my feet tucked into an extra throw. I lie awake, willing myself to fall into the deep folds of sleep. I was once told that it helps to write things down so that the thoughts, plaguing you, are out of your mind and you can rest knowing that, piled onto a piece of paper, they will not be forgotten. Unfortunately, I do not seem to be such a person. The thoughts stick and I lie there planning, arranging, organising all the little inconsequential things that for some inexplicable reason I feel must be done. I always envied my mother for effortlessly letting expectations slide and doing precisely what she felt like doing in any given moment.

Eventually, after twisting and turning, I fall into an alternate universe of shifted experiences, where the most prominent people in my life become heightened personalities, prodding and revealing the fears that I conceal so effectively during the day.

I am at the theatre and our seats are adjacent to the stage, not directly facing the performance. Wedged amongst my family, as large as they are loud, I am twisting back and forth between them and the show. I think it is *The Phantom of the Opera*, but I would not be able to say for sure what it is that we have come to watch. My heart wrenches when I see my beautiful younger sister, Isobel, walking into the theatre with a boy, who, I am sure, I once loved. The feeling, which he did not share, had dissolved into nothingness, but here I am, faced with it yet again. I meet Isobel's eye. She is just like my mother – effortless. Naturally beautiful and fluently re-laxed, she exhibits just the right amount of care for other people without letting it take her over. She looks at me questioningly. Why am I angry? What has she done? We are unable to speak due to the sudden importance of the performance and I turn away.

I wake up. My feet are icy and my shoulders are stiff from their hunched position. I breathe out a shallow sigh of relief that this was just a dream; a distortion of what may be true only in my mind. My hand routinely reaches for the thermometer on my oak nightstand. Pushing it be-tween my lips, I press and wait for the extended beep. The flashing temperature tells me a lot about my body – my cycle, my ovulation pattern, my mood. 36.05 degrees Celsius. I swing my feet out of the bed and I stand and I stretch down, pushing past the dream and past the ques-tions that boldly present themselves every morning. What am I doing with the precious privilege of being alive? Slowly peeling off the carefully assembled layers of sleep, I step out of my box of abstractions into the reali-ties that the daylight presents.

If you walk around Orange Square and take a right turn onto St. Barnabas Street, you will find the small flat I rent. At the suggestion of my brother, William, the re-mains of my college fund were put into an array of funds. It is thanks to the proceeds of these investments that I am able to afford my apartment. Although it feels comforta-ble and cozy during the day, the single-pane windows rat-tle with the wind and let in a distinct chill at night.

Ordinarily, the place is so small that, even when it's tidy, it looks messy. But this morning, my apartment feels light and clean. Small as it is, this space has been care-fully curated over the years. The bedroom opens into both a kitchen nook and a modest living room, cluttered with organization. Books line two of the walls and form perfect piles of wisdom on the floor. An old fireplace, too big for the room, exudes old-fashioned grandeur. A large linen armchair, dented with use, faces an empty loveseat of the same material. When turned on, two gold standing lamps with pale yellow shades weave strands of warm light. A dark, round, chestnut-coloured table glosses in the far corner of the room. The one large window is only half covered by a tilted cotton blind that has been waiting to be fixed for months.

Cushioned in the soft carpet, my bare feet curl their toes. I look out of the window and see mothers in yoga wear as they walk past the church to the market at the end of the road. With a cup of oat coffee I think, I wonder and I contemplate.

The apartment is filled with words: verses and quotes scrawled on receipts, calendar pages, museum fliers, or pages cut adrift from the greatest works of our time. A step into this space means a step into my mind. Dangerous for acquaintances, but beautiful for the initiated. It is almost as if I had scrawled my thoughts and emotions on the walls around me, to guide me back to shore when I become unmoored inside my head. Self-medicating with poetry is my way of connecting to all the souls experiencing the same challenges that I do; we all have felt versions of the same pain. I wonder if poetry could become some sort of universal cure for plaguing feelings, but quickly doubt that the abstractions would be understandable to everybody.

My eyes are pulled away from the words, when I glimpse a childish sketch of the rolling Dorset hills, wedged behind an empty jug and a pile of unread issues of the *Financial Times*. I flick through the headlines, uninterested in their urgency. The subscription is William's, really, though after moving to Frankfurt he had the delivery address changed to mine. Arguably, it was good for me to gain a greater awareness of the ups and downs of the business world. 'Capitalism, and rich employers, who create jobs, are what keep competition and the economy going'. Such is William's response, fervently seconded by my father, whenever my mother and I provocatively discuss the inequalities of income.

It suddenly starts splattering with rain and harsh droplets turn soft onto the double-glazed windows in my living room. So many poets and writers have made the image of racing streams of rain on windows a subject of their analysis. It is a momentary gift of art, only visible to those who look. And only visible for a brief lapse of time, sometimes leaving just the slightest stain or watermark, which is eventually also washed away by the window cleaner on his high ladder.

A father is standing on the cusp of the road with his youngster underneath the globe of a transparent stroller cover. I can't help but long for such shielded ignorance. This little child knows little about the world.

Only following their primal instincts. I feel a pang of anger at myself for not being more grateful for the years of protection my parents similarly offered me. Instead of appreciating it, I had just wafted through bliss, without giving it as much as a second thought.

*

*Ignorance may provide
concealed bliss.*

A freedom of mind.

Kindled thought
roused by
public exchange in text
risks

a broken inward tranquility.

Skepticism,
questioning,
challenging
the accepted.

Thoughts now impossible to ignore.
Participation,
an act of deceit
to one-self.

*

I step into the shower to rinse off. I try to forget about the slight thickening curves beginning to lay themselves over a once much more accepted version of myself. I contemplate last night's dinner, which consisted of German Schnitzel, presumably bought by my mother at the local Bailey and Sage, accompanied by the slightly too sweet roasted vegetables (on their last edible day) with some new potatoes. I say dinner. Really, it was more of an extension of a series of snacks I had consumed throughout the day.

I ask myself almost daily how it can be that there is such a completely clear idea of what should be. Although nowadays you cannot really say the word 'perfect' without getting a tough glance or disapproving look, everyone still strives for perfection. It is utterly superficial and yet something that we almost all intrinsically know and feel. But no, we now live in a world in which billboards are plastered with curvaceous, sexy, womanly figures. And although they are finally up there, I feel that it does not spark a wanting urge for similarity between young women and that person.

I look at it with a subjective inner nod of approval. Well done, it is a step out of the tight lines. But it isn't where it needs to be yet, I remind myself. It is redrawing the lines; a reminder of what *should* be okay but isn't yet. A pitying battle cry against body shaming. How can we determine, dictate and judge certain characteristics to suit a certain assembling of specifically shaped body parts? Our bodies are functioning miracles. A combination of skin, muscle and bone create a vessel for our mind and soul. Together this becomes a person. A human organism with feet and legs to carry them, a middle section perfectly attuned to reproduction, to hold a child safely, to nourish a newborn. And a face with eyes to see, a nose to smell, and a mouth to taste, all the wonders of the planet. This wondrous creation of nature has become an object of scrutiny. Every body part has the right way of being: a 'just right' shape. How can it be that there is a right way for our breasts to sit? For our hair to shine? For our teeth to line up? How can it be that we so easily and readily submit our bodies, which faithfully guide us through life, to this ruthless calculation of beauty? There is a certain extent to which this can be described by general representations of a healthy body or the sensuality that certain curves can trigger. Yet this psychological process by which we do not only harshly judge the color and the shape of ourselves, but actually alter our body with modern technology, is a phenomenon that I will never quite grasp. It strikes me to my core because I think of it my-self. It is an almost inescapable fact of life, which only the fiercest have the strength to avoid.

I was in Paris once, visiting a friend I barely knew, for a weekend in the rain. A small sculpture spotted in a collection of marble slabs and rocky ramekins, assembled in a gallery tucked away from the majestic museums, will always stay with me. The sculpture was soft. I could not really tell if it was a baby or a short, bald woman. All I really knew was that it was a person, with a billowing belly, rounded rolling arms that wrapped their way all-around so that they became a ball of flesh. Eyes closed above full lips and a wide nose; this little figure looked deeply at peace. Not at peace with her figure, but at peace in a way that does not even involve the thought of shape.

I step out of the shower and wrap myself in my warm robe, its belt fitting snugly in-between two squishy roles of belly that indicate the sporadic splurging of the past days.

*

Last afternoon
I played
and
I danced
in the slanted
angles of light,
observing
how their
sharp shades of yellow
touched the soft
c u r v e s
of my

b o d y.
Touching my heart
too.

How beautiful
n a t u r e
is, I thought.

*

After vigorously brushing my teeth with organic grape toothpaste, I down my daily round of supplements, providing my body with the vitamins and minerals it apparently lacks. Next, I walk through the living room to get back to my bedroom. Drawing the curtains, I shake out one or two moths that found their way into the creases of the fabric. I open the window to let the stagnant smell of sleep mingle with the cold air of St. Barnabas Street. Although it is early June, the weather in London remains stubbornly ambivalent. I slightly tilt my chest of drawers to be able to open the built-in cupboards behind them. Underneath an unnervingly humming boiler, I have a few spare shelves in which I keep my tennis gear. I optimistically opt for my white Nike skirt and pull out my K-Swiss tennis shoes. Unable to locate my tennis tops, I put on a long-sleeved, light blue, cotton shirt. Grabbing a banana and my racquet on the way out, I plug my earphones into my outdated phone.

"Take me to the magic of the moment". So cry the Scorpions in 'The Wind of Change', my personal soundtrack as I jog towards Orange Square. I take a right onto Pimlico Road through the neat rows of white homes, as I head in the direction of Warwick Square. I look down into the basement flats to see little pockets of life, glances of families in the midst of a chaotic brunch, or a thought-to-be-alone moment in front of the TV.

Some homes have been luxuriously renovated, but with a conscious effort to keep their original flair. Sometimes this works wonderfully, while in other cases we are left with a protruding glass box, awkwardly jutting out of some part of the kitchen to get more natural light. From the inside, I'm sure the result is spectacular, but on the outside it does rather spoil the appearance of an otherwise perfectly uniform row. But then again, I think, isn't there something to be said for rejecting uniformity and cultivating interior beauty? As so often happens when I start thinking in metaphors, which I usually end up doing at some point in the day, I forget them as soon as I have completed my analysis.

I arrive at Warwick Square a few moments later to find George opening the gates. He read history with some of my friends at Durham before finding work at Mishcon. Now, having been recommended to me by a mutual friend, he makes time to put me through my paces on the tennis court once or twice a week. Although we met as pupil and teacher, a solid friendship grew out of a summer of lessons.

Upon seeing each other, warm smiles spread across both of our faces. The sun breaks through the clouds and I instantly feel at ease. Roots bulge out through the edges of the acrylic mix. Tall trees hang over us, occasionally letting go of a sprinkle of breaking droplets. Forgetting the rummage of thoughts churning in my mind, I give myself up to an hour of the sport. George and I play fiercely, stopping for snippets of conversation over quick sips of water. He taught me my serve, a shortened Andy Roddick version of the classic serve, because I would always open up my racquet too early. I focus on getting into the Nike tick position and, skipping the figure 8 motion, turn the racquet all the way behind my back and slam down a toss that I have refined over the years. We tirelessly chase the ball and sprint back and forth across the court. George catches a ball that was clearly out in the air, silently letting the rally go on. His ball lands in the net a few hits later, and he cries out as though this were naturally my point. Two elderly ladies tentatively mark their arrival and our tennis trance is broken. George wins and we collect the four balls.

"How are you, Clara?" he asks seriously, as we wait at Pimlico Fresh for our lattes and hot sweet cakes to go.

I don't quite know how to respond. Most people wave the trivial question around without expecting a response, but although George is rushing, I know he is asking earnestly. It has always struck me how some people walk past you, saying, 'Hey, how are you?', as though it were simply an extension of a greeting. They are always gone before you even have the chance to respond.

"I'm fine," I opt for in the end, "and you?"

"I'm great. We're working on an interesting intellectual property case at the moment. Bioengineering. It's fascinating, but a lot of material to catch up on."

As we stride back towards his flat on Warwick Square, I sip my second coffee of the day and notice the slightly jittery feeling in my hands that excess caffeine always triggers.

"It's all about this little company, this guy from Imperial, founded just a few weeks ago. He's looking at how stem cells can be used to improve bone growth, mostly to help repair and realign bones after major fractures. I went to see him in his lab a couple of weeks ago and his work is really quite remarkable." He smiles, perhaps registering my caffeinated inattention. "By the way, have you heard anything of Hugo recently? I haven't seen the man in forever and need his input on this."

Hugo is a geneticist at UCL and a good friend of both of ours. He was the one who connected George and myself four years ago. One of those friends who loop in and out of your lives. When present, they burst with energy, but are gone without notice just as often.

"You should invite him to yours tomorrow!" I enthuse.

George has always used the spacious Pimlico apartment given to him by his parents to host small concoctions of people for dinner parties.

"Good idea. I'll give him a call," he replies, as we arrive at his olive-green door. He sticks the greasy bag of cake he is carrying underneath his arm to fish out his keys. His foot is in the door, commitments calling, leaving much more to say in the air.

"Your father never replied to the articles I sent him," I remember.

George's father owns a private equity firm and tends to have the most fascinating views on whatever we talk about. I had sent him some of Frantz Fanon's *The Wretched of the Earth* in response to our last discussion after a lecture in the German Embassy. He had argued that the freelance essay I was currently writing on decolonising curricula had to include reference to some of the atrocities perpetrated by the 'natives' against their own number.

"He never does," George sympathises. "I have to march into his office just to get his attention! He loved seeing you again though. 'Full of energy, passionate and warm', I think he said."

Chapter Two

I am lost. I am so lost. My true response to George's simple question circles my mind, draining and pulling. Further down than many ever reach. I once read that you let the fear, the grief and the ache take over. In 'I Give You Back', Joy Harjo writes:

> *Oh, you have choked me, but I gave you the leash.*
> *You have gutted me, but I gave you the knife.*
> *You have devoured me, but I laid myself across the*
> *fire.*

I wonder if she is right and I am, at least in part, responsible. Unlike Harjo, I have lived a relatively pleasant life. Growing up in a safe and loving environment, I went to bed every night knowing that I was a crucial part of some lives on this planet. The rarity of this was not clear to me at the time, but unavoidably obvious today. If Harjo is right, it would mean that my mind is split and not working as one; that a part of myself is knowingly inflicting misery on itself. The thought is worrying. More so is the fact that the part of me that is bullying the other, seems to be winning.

My grandfather openly and frequently said that members of our family have always been weighed down by a certain *wehmut*[1]. My uncle can remember hearing this at a young age, and though it stayed with him, it does not seem to have marked him. Rather than being weighed

---

[1] 'sadness'

down, I always think of him as light and boisterous. In German I would call him *ein genießer*[2]. Once, when I visited him, we embarked on a discussion of *wehmut* and failure. We spoke about my grandfather's firm values and starkly conservative beliefs. For example, he always insisted that his three children were at home for dinner every night. Now, whilst my parents also always value a family dinner, they are a little more liberal with this rule. My grandfather, however, was uncompromising. Every night the five of them were to sit around the round set table and enjoy a meal cooked by my grandmother. He didn't ask them to help in the kitchen or clean up afterwards. No, he just wanted them there and ready to partake in discussion. And when I see his three children, I see that, whatever it is he was attempting, worked. They are devil's advocates, engaged and passionate speakers interested in almost anything.

I remember spending many afternoons listening to my grandfather read and then writing out German paragraphs to improve my spelling. He would come with a list of topics that he wanted to discuss. But the list was just there for reference, if there was a lack of natural conversation. This was rarely the case and so the list was not always referenced. This sometimes made me anxious. I would ask for the list and would want to go through it with him, quickly if I had to, just to make sure we had covered everything that he wanted to discuss. This is something I often do in life: hastily cover everything, rather than peacefully cover what naturally flows.

I don't know what that list meant to my grandfather, if it included things that he desperately wanted to know or if he simply feared silence. Later, he stopped bringing a

---

[2] 'a connoisseur'

list, or if he did, he didn't have the energy to speak much about whatever was on it. He increasingly spoke about a weight, a sadness, a difficulty with this life that we are living. I must have been oblivious to this when I was younger, but maybe he only showed it to me when he felt I was ready to recognise myself in this emotion. He didn't offer much of a solution to it, nor did he elaborate much on it. I wonder if his *wehmut* had a cause or if it was perfectly inexplicable.

Coming from German nobility, his family's large estate that he was to take over was captured by the Russians. They settled in his beautiful home. As a lover of horses, he stayed and killed them himself to save them from pain. Or to take them from the Russians. He fled to Germany with his family and elderly grandmother. He described his mother, Ama, as the strongest and most powerful woman in the family. Not only for her work to keep the family afloat wherever they went, but for her positivity. She kept the family alive with her smile, her words of wisdom, her safety. Whenever he spoke of her, he smiled.

Our last day together was short and beautiful. My grandfather had stopped fighting his ailments and I had travelled to say goodbye. He took my hand upon my arrival and grasped it very tightly. His hands had always been very cold. "If only for this moment, life was worth living," he said. My eyes glazed with tears, as I attempted to smile. My eyes crinkle when I smile, and he looked at me with a mischievous glint in his eye. "You look Japanese!" These words, coming from his tired soul, made me laugh even more, and I closed my eyes almost completely. I told him I was writing a book and he said, "That doesn't surprise me." I read him some of it and he fell asleep. I asked him for one more quote, but he couldn't muster the strength. I asked my grandmother, who couldn't think of one at that moment. I was desperately trying to cling to something, to some string of words by which I could always remember him. "Bye, my love," he said as he kissed me on both of my cheeks, holding my head in his cold hands.

Cultural rituals and tradition have always been fascinating to me. Often because I perceived them as superfluous. But in the case of my grandfather's funeral I was in awe of the power of coming together. We all shared a connection with the same person, coming together on common ground and celebrating his life as a group rather than individually, let the pain that was hiding come out and be processed together. For some reason, this communal activity, the church, the songs, the food, made it all a little more bearable. The gathering of human contact somehow made his life a little more worthy. The currency of human connection, its value in our society, became so clear to me then. Not as a quantity, like money, but as a quality that shines and highlights a fulfilled life.

Abraham Maslow created a happiness pyramid in which he placed hunger, sex and physiological needs at the bottom. The highest form of happiness is peace with your own self. Possibly like my grandfather – I will never know if so – I am often overcome by a heaviness, indescribable really. An overpowering feeling of not belonging, of somehow being different and apart from others. Without cause and without reason, heaviness settles in my soul and makes itself comfortable. It remains something unspoken. Especially in a family of easy happiness, an unnecessary weight that cannot be explained with a specific cause and effect is not understood.

I wonder why we hide from heaviness. There should always be a reason, a clarity in the pain. That would offer a way out; something to be fixed. But the question remains if that is necessary. Pain and struggle are a part of the beauty of life. The ability to communicate and abstract emotion is a privilege, it is what has set us apart from animals and makes us human. A consistently happy robot would scare us. Sadness is an intricate and necessary element to our souls. And yet we run from it. We hide it from others, and often from ourselves. Every one of our senses is invaluable to our existence. Our senses can overpower and overwhelm us – but how incredible is it that we can feel something, anything, so strongly?

Love, fear, excitement: we are miracle beings, with minds capable of emotion. The greatest freedom can come from completely embracing these feelings. Good or bad, any feeling is something beautiful. Ackermann writes: "It is both our panic and privilege to be mortal and sense-full. We live on the leash of our senses. Although they enlarge us, they also limit and restrain us, but how beautifully". We don't share what drags us down. Just like I didn't share it with George. It is often too complicated to express that adequately in a café or on a quick walk. Unravelling something so big puts a weight on whatever you are doing and people fear that.

Life has become a happiness machine – that is what people strive for and that is what they want to project. I wonder what it would be like if I just shared whatever I was feeling all the time. How would the people around me react? I was told to learn to respond without reactivity. I was once told that reactions and emotions are trains: the earlier you get off and onto the platform, the more control you have. So, I tried jumping off my emotional trains, trying to control the rushing Kings Cross Station in my mind and never quite understood why I couldn't let the trains sit and have a look at what was going on inside of them before shooing them away. "Only necessity is heavy and only what is heavy has value," as Kundera writes.

*

Sometimes
although so safely
cradled
I feel

separate

weighed down
by an emotion

foreign
and unwelcome
with no source
no reason.
A heavy nothingness
expanding in
my soul.

*

I think of summers in Spain, sitting and endlessly staring into nothingness. Feeling overwhelmed with a dragging emptiness that manages to still fill me. In a place objectively luxurious and beautiful, I was filled with pain and for no reason at all. Once, as our boat bobbed along the Mediterranean waves, William had put on 'La Bamba' by Los Lobos and the juxtaposition of its lively melody with my loneliness felt like mockery. Riding the deep blue wave, I felt myself sinking. Not the boat, which sailed its course with ease; nor my body, which was safely ensconced on deck; but my...self...somehow was sinking.

My father turned into our favourite cove, scattered with pockets of life in shining vessels. We slowed to a cruising pace in search of a spot to anchor. Just slow enough to catch a snap of a moment of other lives. Little white boats filled to the brim with fabulously dressed Spaniards and large dark fleets of Rivas or Wally's with a single beauty sunbathing at its tip and a polo-wearing captain behind the glass filled my searching view. A familiar pressing curiosity to know the intricacies of their different lives fought my loneliness. The islands of life nudged me. Reminded me of the passionately different experiences of this life. And the narrow view of experience I so predictably fall into again and again. Surrounded by those who care most, I yearned to be alone. It is paradoxical. William asked me if I was alright. I smiled weakly. "Of course, I am." He knew that I was not, in fact, alright.

I don't know much about the pedagogy of sibling relations. I know that there are different positions that you can be born into, that will go on to shape your persona, your reaction patterns, your confidence and so on. But there are so many factors that play into who it is that you become. I must ask Hugo how much our genetic makeup influences our being and how much is determined by 'nurture'. In any case, I wonder if my restlessness has anything to do with the position that I took in the structure of our family unit. Sandwiched between William and Isobel, two figures of ease and similarity, I sometimes struggle to find common ground. Any person looking in from the outside would not be able to decipher this fact that I have identified over the years. That being said, I don't think that those on the inside would know.

I remember looking into the water, having let the anchor down and facing my rippled reflection. Distorted by the wind-driven crevices in the water, my body was no longer recognisable. I relished the split second in which I saw a version of myself that would have been unrecognisable to any person in my life. Or on this planet. Limbs stretched and rearranged in a way that would no longer be qualified as healthy or normal, if real. It would probably be labelled as disabled or, as they say in Spanish, *minusválidos,* or 'less valid'. I wonder who I would be in this version of myself. How much of who I am today, would be in that person and how much of myself has been shaped by the physically perfected life that I live today? I assume the margin would be wide.

I jumped into the water, my reflection transforming into hundreds of glass-like droplets. Screaming, my head shot back up and out of the water. Tarnished by the tentacles of jellyfish, my skin was burnt and inflamed. I had to swim about 10 metres around the boat, to reach the ladder at the back. My family rushed from all sides, attempting to help. No one was able to pull me up because the edge of the boat was too deep. So I swam. I swam under their watchful gaze, eyeing up the spurts of water that my arms would jerk through, scanning for the jelly like blobs. I myself could not see what was ahead, I could only prepare myself for another sting. But with their help I circumvented more pain and managed to get out of the water without another burn.

They huddled around me, sharing my anguish. My mother wrapped me in a soft yellow towel and my father, already with the first aid kit in hand, immediately sprayed my leg with the prescribed antidote. I stood there burning with excruciating tingles of pain and covered with love. And although they were there and they were fussing over me, my loneliness persisted. It was me who felt the sting and no matter how much they cared for me, only I could experience that sensation. And yet I was thankful for having that kindness around me; the hopeless attempt to alleviate the pain.

*

Island Summer

Empty cloud
adrift
in the summer sky.

Overripe tomatoes
not picked
pressed to dry dirt.

A distant flat ocean
baking
in the slow sun.

Days roll into
months of
unrevolutionary summers.

Distant dreams
untouched hearts
fading
mixing
with simple happiness.

Chapter Three

I arrive at George's the next day and, after a quick kiss on the cheek, rush right into the guest bathroom. Annoyed at myself for wasting a bathroom getaway right at the start, I relieve my bladder.

When I come out, I hover in the doorway, where I can see the others standing around George who is finishing off a salad. Hugo is making a salad dressing and his girlfriend, Julia, is helping him. She is wearing a cream costume set and he is wearing a shirt under a cashmere sweater with chinos and brogues. Richard, an old friend of George's from Eton, is already sitting at the table drinking wine. In the corner of the room is a man I have never met before, who later introduces himself as Arthur. His hands are covered in a white clay-like residue and his clothes are beautifully ruined. Our eyes skim past each other, a brief fixation powerfully distracting. The promise of something more in a glance has often occurred in my lifetime and yielded little. I am snapped out of my reverie by the sound of George's voice. Already, even this early in the evening, he is convening a discussion on education.

"What do you think," he asks, "about abolishing grammar schools?"

"I'm not sure," Arthur replies. "They're good for the children whose parents couldn't afford to send them to Eton, like ours did."

"The reason I ask is because a client recently told me he believes grammar schools take funding away from other schools, which equally need support."

"I don't think grammar schools should be abolished," Richard interjects. Loudly. "I think it's only right that the smartest kids can go somewhere that will allow them to reach their potential." He is almost sputtering now. "How the Hell are they meant to do that in a comprehensive where the level is set for the benefit of the lowest common denominator?!"

"What nonsense!" The force of my opinion practically moves me bodily from my position in the doorway, prompting me to make a rather bolder entry into the room than I had intended. "Grammar schools are just an excuse to let comprehensive schools off the hook. If 'the smartest kids' all go to grammars, then why would comprehensives ever raise expectations and encourage all students to reach their potentials?"

"Ah! Clara, hello hello. I was waiting for your view on this." Hugo embraces me and I give Julia a kiss on the cheek. Arthur walks over and I am able to study him properly for the first time. He has rugged dark brown hair and is the tallest man in the room. Wearing loose fitted linen trousers, a white t-shirt, and worn trainers, he is also dressed the most casually.

"Lovely to meet you," he says, warmly. "I'm Arthur."

"I'm Clara."

Richard gives me a quick kiss on each cheek before returning, undeterred, to his argument. "I do see your point, Clara, but I don't think the right solution is to get rid of the advantages that grammar schools provide. Comprehensives should be encouraged to improve, and provided with the resources to do so, rather than just bringing the top students down, which is precisely what abolishing grammar schools would do in my opinion."

"Inequality will always exist," says George, as he swoops in and pours me a glass of red Mallorcan wine.

As he does so, I notice the beautifully inscribed label of our friends' vineyard: *ses Tallioles*. "But surely," he continues, "is lowering the quality of the best education providers worse than raising the quality of the worst education? Otherwise, we should abolish all private schools too!"

"We are so lucky," I intervene. "Our whole worldview – or part of our worldview – is shaped by the fact that we have been born into such exorbitant privilege. I don't mean to say that we are all billionaires with luxury yachts. But when you look at our homes, our parents, the holidays we enjoy, the wine we drink..." Here, I raise my glass, as if I were toasting our advantages. "In terms of our family backgrounds and our material comforts, we are leaps and bounds ahead of most people. But is it really fair? Maybe instead of chewing over the rights and wrongs of education systems we should get stuck in ourselves. Do some teaching."

"I would just make everything much more independent," replies Arthur, offering a compromise. "The way that things were done at Eton – I mean, there were entire societies where the dinners and events were just organized by the students. The teachers did nothing! Which meant that we learned both independence and teamwork. Surely instilling such values is better than simply telling students what to think so they can pass an exam?" Considering his argument, I look at him and wonder why I have never met him before.

Arthur's memories of Eton push political considerations to one side as the boys begin to reminisce.

"I had this one teacher at Arnold House," George recollects, "Year 5, I think, so I must have been 8 or 9. Or pushing 10. He inspired my interest in Geography. And Geology. Thanks to him, by the time I moved schools I was years ahead of everybody else. Funny how a teacher can impact your life and stick in your mind years later. I can still see him, he was this huge guy, with a bright red face."

"And I'm sure he drank like a fish," replies Arthur, raising his glass. His eyes shine with passion whenever he partakes in the discussion. Most of the time he observes and then when asked something, he would open up into lengthy monologues with such specific knowledge that people can contribute little and simply sit and listen, with fascination. I wonder how he knows so much and how he remembers it all. Catching my eye, we stare at each other a little longer than the first passing glance. It reminds me of the feeling when you spot someone attractive on the tube and daringly lock eyes, although everything inside you is willing you to look away. When both people do this, it can be more powerful than any exchange of words. Then one person usually gets out at the next stop and you are left thinking, what if? What if I had said something? How would the fate of my life have changed?

Arthur gets out a little note pad and starts scribbling something, deeply concentrated.

"Inspiration must have hit him," whispers Julia as she leans over to me. "Have you ever seen his work?"

"No, I haven't. What is it like?"

"Really? Oh, he's quite a famous fellow, actually. Just had an exhibition at the Saatchi Gallery. Wait, I'll show you." She takes out her phone and googles his name. Even on such a small screen I am transfixed by what I see. Stunning sketches and sculptures of women in different shades of clay. I am lost in a sea of beauty, entranced, letting the other voices breeze past.

"I'm sure he did!" Absentmindedly, I can hear George in full conversational flight. "When we were reciting nouns, he would punch the bookcase!"

"I had a similar chap at Charterhouse called Mr. Brisbane. Fantastic Latin master. He would read us Greek mythology on Saturdays. I suppose it was more of a passive education. We didn't quite switch off, just listened to stories of Persephone, Demeter, and Hades, as if they had lived in the same surroundings in which we found ourselves."

The exchange of old school stories sparks excitement in the boys and we forget where the conversation started. We settle into what is comfortable and try to push away what would make us ignorant of what needs to be changed. I go along with it.

At the end of the night I stand at the sink and wash up some of the dishes, so that George doesn't have to stay up all night after we leave. Arthur comes up to me and takes the salad bowl out of my hands to dry with a cloth. After a while of silently standing next to each other, smiling every now and then, softly nudging our shoulders against each other he speaks with grounding confidence.

"I'd love to see you again."

"So would I." The words rush out a little too fast.

"Let's go on a walk around London tomorrow, when it's completely and utterly quiet."

"I'd like that."

The others call an uber to go to the Cock and Bottle on Westbourne Grove for a pint, but feeling the wave of thoughts starting to hit I go home.

*

*What sweet pleasure
can be derived,*

*conjecturing how best
to attempt
contriving how best
to convince
the early moments of
promising acquaintance.
Idle possibilities
tempt
the innocent mind.*

*A plunging line
delicately retraced
cautious not to flail
concealing sentiment.*

*Playful ruptures
teasing rhetoric
kindling exchanges
consume and
intrigue.*

*A brief touch
a momentarily prolonged glance
deep into what resides
beyond the exterior.*

*Blossoming flirtation,
a fragile affair.*

Chapter Four

I walk home, listening to The Corrs sing 'When The Stars Go Blue'. "Where do you go when you're lonely? / I'll follow you." My mind conjures images of Arthur. I dream of something that I know has happened and does happen to many. Falling in love. For some reason that is unknown to me, I have not experienced true romantic love yet. I have yet to fall into the power of what so many people have endlessly chronicled in songs, poetry, novels, and any other form of expression. I think that sometimes I have cheated on love itself by attempting to simulate or force myself to feel something I simply didn't. Not that I know what that would feel like. I wonder if this tingling is some kind of indication of a beginning, or if Arthur is just another simulation.

Suddenly a fox crosses the road and a lady's dog races after it. She screams and chases it, but has no chance of catching up. Devastated, she ends up standing, tension in every muscle, straining to see and waiting for her dog to return.

Somehow tarnished by most of my past experiences with men, I tentatively push the dreaming clouds of fantasy away. I do not know Arthur enough to want him, I remind myself. I sometimes wonder why love comes so easily to some and why I seem to push and tug at it in all the wrong ways. Throughout my life, I was always surrounded by familial love. My parents were in love with each other and in love with their children. My grandparents were in love with each other and in love with their children and grandchildren. Generations of love built the foundations of our family. The love of my family gave me a solid support and a safety net that I always knew was there. Even if we did not need it, knowing that it was there, gave us the courage and confidence to take risks and do things that people without a safety net, without that love, might not.

I think of inequalities and of the simplest privilege of being loved. Last weekend my father had looked at me with glowing eyes, still in his damp tennis clothes, rain against the window, mixing with the sun and reflecting an infinite number of multicolored strands of light through the room. "Often, I just stop what I am doing and think of how proud I am of you" he said, "I do this so many times throughout the day."

Looking up at him from the yellow velvet armchair that I was wedged in, I close my book. "Thank you Papi, I love you." His eyes are glassy now and he looks out of the window "I am serious Clara. What you are doing with your life, the people you touch, your beautiful, strong heart. You have the same smile that you had as a little girl."

I wanted to go up and squeeze him and tell him how much I love and admire him. I thought of the many people that I have met without such loving fathers. I thought of the many successes that he has had in his life; that he has every right to be a little too confident or a little too busy. He was there for every problem that I have ever had; every thought that I wanted to share, proudly and strongly standing by Mami's side and teaching us to value and respect every person that we meet, no matter their background. I think of many things in that moment: memories of swinging in his arms or racing him up a hill or him, teaching me how to serve or us weighing the pros and cons of every single important decision of my life, but I can't explain any of it.

The words for the magnitude of my gratitude didn't appear, so I didn't say anything. I smiled softly again, and he walked away, smiling too. I turned back to my book, but the rush of emotion stopped me from focusing on the words of those pages. My eyes were wet and the words swimming. I looked out through the multicolored rain droplets into the sun. At this moment I feared so much. That I have not shown him how much I admire him; that I have not told him every day how much I love him. That I have something very big to lose. And so I sat there, brimming with a complex blend of emotion. Strong, deep love and sudden, excruciatingly obvious fear.

Growing up, my father always told us that there is no greater success in life than achieving a state of happiness. Although I find the pursuit of constant happiness slightly unrealistic and not an accurate depiction of emotive life, I think that he was alluding to a deeper sense of appeasement. I think that he was alluding to love. I wonder then why I have pushed most pursuers away, preferring instead to chase the impossible candidates of unavailability, knowing that they would falter too. But something had stirred in me tonight, something bigger than a preconceived failing attempt to love. I like him, I think.

Mozart's 'Elvira Madigan' begins to fill my ears and I revel in the beauty of it. I should know more about music, given the fact that I grew up in a family in which every and any extracurricular activity would have been cheered on, financially and motivationally. And yet I chose to bask in the ease of doing nothing. I think of what I felt when I graduated from university and remember the sense of completion and mild satisfaction. I had studied Anthropology and found it interesting, but it had not gripped me and it had not pushed me to my edge. I doubt that in an alternate universe, in which we follow our truest desires, I would have chosen to spend three years of my academic life in those rooms. But it wasn't Finance or Business, which I would have been even less inclined to enjoy.

So, I had pushed the boundaries a little, but still I felt mild satisfaction. I felt that *I chose to bask in the ease of doing nothing.* This is not something intrinsically negative, and yet it is commonly perceived as such. But I must say, it is very easy to conceal. As are most of the shortcuts that I have taken in life. My therapist might say that only I would define these routes as shortcuts. I grew up in a family of performers. Normal was not a standard. Although never pushed, it was as though there was an invisible force that nudged us in a direction of expectation. My siblings shuffle around, have fun, and are natural talents in all that they strive to be. It is wondrous to witness. A balance between uncomplicatedness and success, that I will forever be trying to replicate.

My older brother stepped into the successfully trodden corporate footsteps of my father. Eternally loved by my father, my mother raised our family and, on the side, helped every person who crossed her path with vigorous enthusiasm. My younger sister Isobel was something else. A standard that I would never reach, her bubbling beauty and ease of life matched that of my mother. It is the *ease* that fixated my mind for most of my childhood. I was perplexed, that life and joy could come so easily to them. She does not care about so much of what I obsess over. She would leave her suitcase untouched for weeks on end in the midst of her disaster of a room after a holiday. And instead of mocking this, I admired it. How relaxed do you have to be to let that go? For me that is impossible. Clean room, clean mind, I know. But her mind can be clean, without the clean room.

I felt that as the older sister I was the experimenter for life's tests. I would share what worked, what didn't, and Isobel would take a secure path that had been trodden before, whilst I was already grappling with the next unknown. For years I idealised her to the point that I could not see her. I could not see that all she wanted was to be my friend. I fought and judged myself. I remember sometimes going to bed at night and going through every part of my body challenging it, perfecting it in my mind. And all the while she looked up to me. Around the age of sixteen, I finally realised that her support and love for me was unwavering. I realised that I had to let go of the relentless game of comparison and exchange it for her love.

Once I did that, a whole new world opened to me. I still fought myself, but I no longer fought her. She became and is the person that knows me better than anybody else on this planet. Every single thing, every detail of my life, my thought process and my fears are tucked into her soul. No matter how lost I am, she knows what to say to pull me out of my mind.

And yet there is a gap. An element of her that I will never be able to reach. Unlike me, a relatively open book and a face that instantly reveals the emotions going on inside of me, she is mysterious. Beautifully mysterious. Something I think that enraptures the people around her and makes them want to know and find out what is going on in her mind for themselves.

Chapter Five

It is 11 p.m. the next day and I am waiting by the mag-
nolia, in front of Arthur's large, white, Victorian home
when he comes running up with two paper bags and two
takeaway coffee cups in his hands. He looks even better
than the image I had drawn in my mind after yesterday.
My heart skips a little. I am nervous that I may have mis-
understood, that this is just a friendly meeting, already
knowing that even if it isn't, any feelings I have now
could just as easily dissipate into nothing as fast as they
have arisen.

"Hello! Hello! Sorry I'm late. I've just been to get the
essentials...coffee and bacon! Are you hungry?"

We embrace and I get a whiff of the delicious bacon
rolls and earthy coffee.

"Famished! I haven't eaten a thing since lunch. After
last night I'll definitely need some coffee to keep these
sleepy eyes open. I almost fell asleep on the tube this
morning, albeit only for a moment or two."

Arthur has to rattle the key in the lock a bit to open the
door, laughing as he does so.

"Clara." His eyes crinkle with laughter. "There is no
way that's how you've pronounced 'albeit' all your life!"

"What do you mean?!"

"*All-be-it*," he corrects, "not *ahl-beyt*."

"How is it *all-be-it*?! Where are the spaces?!"

"You're right! Where the hell are the spaces? All. Be.
It. It's very deceptive. I used to live in Hamburg and my
roommates always took the piss out of me because I
couldn't pronounce the word 'Huenchen' and said
'huenhuen' instead!"

"Well, I always used to say *earl*, instead of *u-r-l*."

"No way! I'm desperate to find a website that will help me learn German properly. Clara, if you know of one, please can you send me the *earl*?!"

"Shut up!" I playfully push him away.

"Okay, okay. So, you took the tube this morning, didn't you? Thank goodness I don't have to commute. My journey this morning was from my bed to my slippers and then to the kitchen."

"You're lucky. The tube was horrible. I could barely even sit down. I swear, every time I did, someone nearby would cough and sneeze so I had to get up and move! It was like musical chairs."

"Normally, I do almost all of my work in Dorset. The city has too many distractions. The piano tuner was here today and I almost went insane. The same note over and over again. Usually I can only stick it out in London for a few days at a time."

The house is beautiful. A huge old wooden spiraled staircase curls its way up through the middle of the house, opening up to a view into all of its different layers. Pieces of antique furniture collected over years are tucked into every nook. The walls are covered in art, old and new. But no sculptures and no paintings that I would recognize as his.

I wonder where he keeps his work. Yellow wallpaper is peeling off the walls of a cluttered kitchen. Different jars with all sorts of spices and herbs are stacked against each other. Arthur opens an ancient fridge, which is filled to the brim with boxes and boxes of food all busily culti- vating new life. The smell of fermenting kimchi, bottled gherkins and moulding cheeses hits me. He gets out a glass bottle of milk and pours some into the paper cups of coffee. I awkwardly follow him, not sure what to do with myself in his attuned habitat. As if reading my mind, he leads me back outside, onto neutral ground. We catch the last slice of cool, dry air before the forecasted rain hits.

"I feel like there are a million stories to be told about everything that's been collected in that house over the years."

"I'm very lucky to stay in it. My parents spend most of their time in South America nowadays, and the few times a year that they do come to the UK, they like to stay at our home in Dorset."

We pause to take in the beauty of the night. There is something special about walking over streets that are normally hustling and bustling with people, so empty.

We walk and we talk for hours. Well, for the most part I listen while Arthur talks, slowly unpeeling the layers of knowledge he has wrapped up inside him. He tells me about the buildings we pass, or what once stood in their place. Who lived where, what they achieved. So many of the scientists and philosophers who have shaped our worldview. He is in his element, explaining something that only a few people would even listen to. I am enraptured by his enthusiasm. An artist reading about economics, or genetics, or quantum physics? How this makes sense is a mystery to me, but beautiful. It is what I strive to do. To look at the world in a holistic way, without the cutting edges of borders and boxes.

Every now and then he takes out his notebook and discreetly scribbles or sketches something. I wonder what it is that pops into his mind at those random moments, but I don't ask. The less he reveals, the more I can wonder.

*

49

The mingling of
souls
opens up to
a trifling tweeze
or a
tormenting twist,
churning sentiment.

Given easily
and
received tragically
it is
inevitable
in
depth.

*

Eventually, we end up at his doorstep and sit down on the steps.

"Do you believe in fate? Or star signs?" I look up as I speak.

"Of course I do. The big bang was so particular and so intended. It was an exact number and ratio of atoms and particles that needed to collide with each other, and I feel that these sequences of numbers present themselves in our lives today. I watch out for the patterns, in birthdays and star signs. I do believe in astrology and the energies of the moon, stars and their influence on us. But I still believe that we can control our actions, in the same way that we can combine numbers in the way that we want."

I have never thought about it like that and don't think I will ever be a person who looks out for numbers. But still it fascinates me and I study his face.

"I'm leaving for Dorset tomorrow. I just have to get back out to my studio. I've been working on a big project, for a year now and I think I'm very close to the finish line." As he speaks, he looks at me, closely.

"I'd love to see some of your pieces...in the flesh, so to speak."

We pause and a quiet settles over us.

"Why don't you join us next week? I've invited the boys, Hugo, George, Richard and his twin brother Mark. They're all coming down for a few days of hunting. Squirrels, mostly, maybe some bucks. It might help you reconnect with nature, or to escape into a different world! You could come up a day earlier than the others and enjoy some peace and quiet."

His offer surprises me. I hadn't pegged him as a man who plays with girls, casually inviting them on weekends of pleasure. Nor did his behaviour suggest he was love-struck with me and ready to drop everything for a week-end away. Whatever the case, it has happened more quickly than I expected. I feel myself preparing to decline, finding the thought of the weekend I had already planned for myself to be the easier option. The safer option. But then I think of the coast, the fields, the leaves on the trees, and the peacefulness of it all seduces me. I nod my acceptance and want to kiss him, searching his face for a clue, some indicative movement I could take as my cue to lean in. But it doesn't happen.

Already, I am mentally rearranging the piled dinner plans, coffee commitments and lunch dates with visiting friends. I leave feeling understood, although we do not speak about anything particularly confusing to me. Arthur is interested in studying the intricacies of the world. And whatever those may be, however niche, that fundamental curiosity is the most important quality there is to me.

Chapter Six

I wake up late and am reminded of last night with a jolt of tingling happiness. I go over everything, every detail and every look that I can remember. Thinking of his smile I brush my teeth and get dressed, very pleased that I have the distraction of meeting my mother for an early lunch to take my mind off Arthur. I pull on loose fitted jeans and a blue cashmere sweater, with a pair of orange ballerinas. Scraping my blonde hair into a messy bun, I wash my face and stop to stare at my own reflection in the small wooden-framed mirror of my bathroom. My eyes, alight from last night, look back at me, shining with daring hope. My heart skips a little and I feel happy. Excited for what is to come. I keep looking until I reach that point where your own face looks alien to you, and you begin to wonder why it is that we have a nose jutting out the middle of your face with two holes. My face begins to dry up and I push out of my mini trance and back into the real world of noses, eyes and mouths.

We have a reservation at Iddu, just off South Ken station. I decide to walk the thirty minutes through the backstreets of Chelsea it takes to get there. She is sitting outside at a round tiled table and has already ordered our usual pistachio pesto pasta with a side of garden salad to share. My mother is a beautiful woman with a smile that reaches every single person. A ray of sunshine and a bundle of energy, dressed in a white blouse and a soft yellow cardigan. My father would pride himself in saying that, no matter how boring a business function would be, he knew that if he took my mother, she would lighten it up and get a story out of even the most earnest businessman.

When I was going through high school my mother was a constant and reassuring presence, always by our side. I was an emotional child, and I weighed up everything that people said, or every look they gave, and brought it home to dissect. It was our grade that had all the classic beauties. They formed a clique, and I wondered why it is that the smart and beautiful often found each other to form an alliance. William used to tell me he was set up for success because of his height. If you are 2 metres everyone looks up to you. Although I half-heartedly belonged to this clique, it was never the same for me. I am not sure if this is because I was emotionally torn and unable to fully give myself to the gossip and teenage drama or if I was ever so slightly excluded due to external factors.

My mother had never worn a speck of makeup herself and unwillingly following suit, me and Isobel ended up being the last in our year groups to wear mascara. And when we finally did, in the 10th grade, it was dubiously applied in inexperienced clumpy globs, weighing down our eyelids and subject to the scrutiny of at this point experts, wearing dainty, high quality, carefully applied product.

Possibly more embarrassing, was the fact that we were also the last to wear a bra. My mother was not neglecting us, on the contrary, all she wanted to do was being with us, but was neglecting the beauty standards of the 21st century. So, nipples out until the 9th grade and wearing red corduroy trousers with enthusiastically acquired second-hand Hollister tops from our friends, we walked the high school hallways.

It wasn't that my mother didn't want us to have certain things (although she hated leggings or anything lacy) but she wanted us not to *care* about these things. At that point it could be painful, being the last in the year to wear leggings under denim shorts, but today I look back in wonder. She never cared about these things, not her whole life. What power must you need to *not care* about things that everyone else obsesses over?

No matter how superficial it seems in retrospect, it never was at the time. In winter she would pick us up from school in our VW, kitted out with snow suits, flasks of hot chocolate and wrapped up sandwiches, piling us in and driving up to the closest sledging hill. We would groan a little at the start but then an hour later with wind in our hair and cold, rosy cheeks we would be a giggling heap of happiness. In summer, she would blow up the pool in our garden and after picking fresh plums or apples, bake one crumble after another, until we could not eat one more piece of crumbly cake. I was mildly happy in my half-belonging state at middle school and would come home to a place in which I could completely belong. Our home was a haven of sunshine and I would race out of my last period to meet my mother, leaving the superficial hallway talk far behind and not thinking of it until anxiously awaiting it the next morning.

My family remained the epicentre of my life. In my final school years, I grew into part of the person that I am today. I met my first boyfriend; albeit not my one true love it was a first signal of desirability. My confidence grew ever so slightly. And I flourished ever so slightly. I met my closest friend; a sincere friendship grounded in shared values and kindness. Slowly the confidence to be honest about who I was as a person, grew inside of me. What I was proud of and what I needed to work on. This step in honesty, between myself and others, was the biggest step thus far in my life to becoming a critical thinker. It was only when I learnt that if I viewed the difficulties of my own life as something to be recognized and ana-lysed as some sort of experiment, that I realised all of our experiences on this earth are an incredible disarray of ups and downs. Ups and downs based on some sort of social strata that will always remain impossible to please. This realisation came to liberate my ever-attempting soul.

Released from this socially induced fear of hiding fail-ure, I began walking through life with a sense of, at times annoyingly open, recognition of flaws. That does not mean that I accepted these flaws or quirks in my path, if you will. On the contrary, quite like at school I remained deeply emotion-driven, liable to the painful boxing-in of right and wrong. But now I was aware of the origin of my pain. I know now that I am a person in the midst of social construction. And being aware helps, because there is al-ways a small voice inside of me reminding me to let go of the force, to not give in. To carve out my own version of this life that we are living.

"I've started to learn Portuguese!" Such *non-sequiturs* and exciting pronouncements are not uncommon when talking to my mother. "The accent is so nasal, I'm pretty sure I need to wear a washing peg on my nose to get it just right!"

She starts speaking in a Portuguese accent, which makes me think of summers spent in different countries. On family holidays, my mother would always try to learn the language, and usually make a decent fist of it, but more often than not she would simply imitate the accent. It was as though she thought this would allow the locals to understand her better. It's rather endearing, but also a little patronizing, albeit unintentionally.

We talk about the family foundation and how best to employ the money that is in the fund. She is undecided if she should invest in one cause and only one cause, essentially increasing her impact by funneling more resources into a targeted issue. This is rationally the right choice, but my mother helps every person that turns up on her doorstep. Literally. Recently a blind man came by to sell scissors and other miscellaneous objects that we did not need. Instead of just sending him away or buying one thing to shut him up, she invited him inside and had coffee with him. She found out that he was a piano tuner before he became homeless. She employed him to regularly come and tune our piano. A little step into a sustainable future for him. She pitches that the motto of our fund should be "random acts of kindness". Understandably, she does not want to limit herself to a set cause, because she so passionately wants to help people in her vicinity. Although, technically speaking, the money would probably have a more dramatic impact on the war in Syria or the refugee camps in Uganda. There are so many theoretical mind games that present this moral dilemma. Do you save the child or the Picasso in a burning house? No matter how many children could be saved with the money made by selling the Picasso, my mother would always save the child. The Picasso would not even cross her mind.

I was once told that if you want to understand pretty much ninety-five per cent of everything that happens, you only have to understand two things. One is Darwin's theory of evolution (just clock that one) and the second is Game Theory. Altruism is never purely altruism. Altruism is a social contract you enter into because you think it's better for you genetically. For the most part we function as a society, not because we believe in society, but because we think our individual chance is increased through that construct. You can see that most societies actually work when looking at the numbers. They tend to map that very well, so most people go along with the rules because otherwise it breaks down. But in that context, a small percentage can cheat and be very successful as cheaters, if the majority adheres to the rules. Adhere to the rules and believe that you're adhering to the rules. As soon as that cheating number gets too high, the construct falls apart, and you have to restart. Everyone has a game strategy, in order to actually genetically succeed. Social altruistic, ideas of good and bad, are fundamentally just different approaches to the complex nature of interactions.

Although it is harsh, why you truly do something is normally very hard to know because often altruistic acts are done instinctively. You don't sit there and calculate. It's an intrinsic pattern in your behaviour which is learnt. My mother, by investing the foundation trust into individual people that she randomly comes into contact with, is not effective altruism. The money could be invested in stocks, then sold and given to a hunger crisis, to be most effective all at once. It would not be very rewarding, maybe that one transfer moment would feel good but it would not be a task with a process and result because of her time and effort. I am similar to my mother and wonder what I would be doing if I had to decide how best to give and serve those less fortunate. I would probably do the same. I think.

Maybe if you truly love someone you might quite purely do something beyond yourself. But then again, isn't it the biggest pleasure there is on this earth to love and be loved? So maybe, those acts too have been naturally selected to serve yourself.

*

Isobel joins us for an espresso and the famous almond biscotti at an Italian cafe across the street. She crosses the street in a wispy red wrap-dress, tied around the waist. Her dirty blonde hair frames her radiating face in the wind.

"Hola chicas!" She shouts from across the street, running a little to catch up with the words already reaching us. My mother and I wave. It is one of those moments where, if you do not know the person that you are meeting very well, it feels as though you have to wait an eternity awkwardly smiling at each other, until one person manages to cross the street safely.

"I missed you!" she exclaims, finally having arrived and falling straight into my mother's arms. The line behind looks at us uncomfortably, as though one person more means we should be retreating to the back of the line.

"I missed you too!" I give her two kisses on the cheek and cannot help but notice how beautiful she looks. "You look amazing!"

"Ugh! No, no, I've been eating so much. You have no idea. And drinking too!"

"Well, I can't see it on you!"

"You can never see it on me!" And like that my compliment isn't really a compliment anymore. It is difficult to make one without insinuating any form of comparison.

"I think you both look amazing! I am so proud of my girls." Our mother swoops in and puts both her arms around us. The line always moves a little quicker than expected at this place and before we know it, it's our turn.

After we order, I smile brightly at the cashiers bored face. Sometimes I do that: I am annoyingly smiley just to see how people will react. Usually I get a delayed smile. This time it's a look of nothing. Boredom.

"Do you think everyone finds the same things boring?" I ask as we walk towards a wooden ridged bench. We sip our hot lattes and I close my eyes, turning my face right into the sun. The hotness seeps into my already paling skin and paradoxically the cancerous rays rejuvenate me.

"I don't think so. A lot of the kids I help out, would be perfectly happy working at Sainsburys or McDonalds one day." My mother is one of those people that loves any sort of discussion, any deeper question but will usually participate on the basis of her individual experiences. And yet, she always makes a point, which few do well.

"That's not what I mean. They would be happy to get a job like that because of the stability it would provide. I doubt that they would actually enjoy it."

Isobel takes a bite of my mother's croissant and starts speaking "I mean...to be honest, Clara, I feel like you would sit at the Sainsbury's counter and start analysing all of the different customers..."

"I wish!" I laugh. "But I'm not that curious, Iso. I find that interesting for an hour, two at most, but then I'd get bored. I was recently in town with some school friends who wanted to go shopping."

"But you hate shopping!" Mami exclaims.

"I know, but I thought I would just go along as Floss had just been paid and wanted some company. I ended up getting something at each shop we went into. And when I got home, I tried it all on and it just didn't look right. I looked through my already endlessly cleared out closet and once again was hit but how much stuff I have. Stuff that I don't need!"

"What's your point, Clara?" Isobel asks.

"I'm getting there! I ended up going back to each store and returning everything except for a white t-shirt that I actually needed. My point is, I was standing in these end-less return lines and was observing all of these people, mostly women, buying into consumerism and marketing and capitalism. Colours, slogans, catchy alliterations, all of these tools to lure people's senses. I was standing there and I couldn't believe what I was seeing. I couldn't be-lieve that I'd fallen victim to it just a few hours ago."

"That's a bit dramatic, Clara. What do you mean with fallen victim to?" My mother prods.

"It's not dramatic! I genuinely stood there thinking: Wow! Why is this woman in front of me buying a cheaply manufactured pleather tote for 90 pounds? And two sets of earrings, gold and silver hoops. And then I started an-alysing everyone and everything that they were carrying and I just couldn't believe that they spend their days at work boring themselves for the most part and then spend-ing the money that they make, boring themselves, on a pleather bag! What kind of logic is that? It's not like they were buying functional things. They were buying extras."

"Yes, Clara, that's fashion," says Isobel. "Just because we got to steal most of our stuff from Mami or Omi doesn't mean others just get all these things that make us happy too." She tugs at my blue sweater that I had in fact gotten from Mami after Ivanka had shrunk it.

"True. Anyways, that was what you meant in terms of observing, I think. But I could do that for an hour of re-turns and after forty-five minutes, I was so annoyed at standing in that line that I swore to myself, to just know now, that I am not a shopper and to stop wasting money on stuff I don't need. I wouldn't be able to stand there watching all day long as a cashier. I'd go crazy."

"Well yes, I guess people do find most of these jobs boring," she agrees.

"I guess. We do them because we have to."

"And a small percentage of us have the privilege of an intellectually challenging profession," my mother interjects.

"That doesn't necessarily need to be a privilege," I start. "What about teachers?"

"What about them?" Isobel asks.

"Teachers are most commonly not from the upper, upper class and yet they have an intellectually stimulating profession. It is definitely not a *boring* job."

"A lot of people don't share that opinion. Whilst important, teaching is often interpreted as quite repetitive or basic, don't you think?" Isobel comments.

"I guess. I don't agree."

"I know you don't." My mother starts looking at me with a shifted expression on her face, as though she can see my life unfolding before her eyes.

"What's up? Why are you looking at me like that?" I ask.

"I'm just thinking what you two girls are going to do one day. I'm so excited. It's like watching a movie."

"Except not really," Isobel laughs. "Mami! This is our life. You have to get nice and involved, not just let the movie have any old ending."

"I don't think you need my help. Would you have actually liked it, if your father and I said you'll get a large sum of money, just like that once you are done with university?"

"That's not what I was talking about, but yeah I guess sometimes I don't think I'd complain about it," Isobel jokes.

"I'm actually quite unsure about that question," I add. "I have so many friends that are cushioned their whole lives and it does not affect their perseverance to perform and prove themselves. I would almost argue they can be even more daring, as they have little to lose."

"But that is not how the real-world works. Wouldn't it be more important for you to have an authentic experience of life?"

"Is that what is most important? Authenticity?" I ask.

"I think so. Otherwise you don't really live honestly." Isobel smiles. "But then again that line is so blurred. Is our life thus far authentic?"

"No, it isn't. You kids grew up with standards up here." My mother points to the sky. "And you need to get used to going down a little."

Isobel laughs loudly and nudges me "Thanks for the vote of confidence, Mami! I can already see us girls here in a few years earning peanuts and William breezing through the good life."

"'The good life'," I repeat out loud, without knowing why. Sometimes I do that to just feel the words in my mouth. Repeating them to myself, as though the deeper meaning might reveal itself that way.

"Yeah. Been pretty good, so far," Isobel sighs and we sip our drinks.

After a while I speak. "As long as it doesn't get boring. That would really mean going down to me."

"What do you think you could do that you wouldn't find boring?" Mami asks.

I think and don't reply right away. In fact, I wait for so long that I can already hear the intake of her breath as if to ask a follow up question. I quite like silences when people speak. It adds such drama and provides a moment for reflection within whatever you are discussing.

I stop her from interjecting. "Firstly, you would obviously already know if I had an answer to that question."

"I know, I know."

63

"It just has to be something analytical. I'm an over-thinker. I want to use that to do something good. And I want to do something where I'm not bored, where I don't count down the hours."

"You'll find the right thing." My mother looks at me lovingly.

"If not, we can always go to the Hamptons and be yoga teachers!" Isobel laughs.

The heaviness of the conversation leaves and is replaced with a lightness. I sit wedged between these two incredible women who support me with everything that they have and an overwhelming happiness overcomes me. It is impossible to put into words (I feel protected and safe and loved) it overwhelms me and I can't think about it properly. This feeling is different to the usual peace of everyday happiness.

When I leave, I look at Mami, already missing her. I think of our conversations, of boredom and of time. My entire life I have struggled with the idea of time. Even in my gap year I would count down the weeks of whatever I was doing, an internship, a trip, volunteering. I think of the date with an Italian boy which made this issue so obvious to myself, that I knew I had to work on it. After a couple of standard dinner and drink dates, we had progressed to an evening in my first city flat. Alberto was his name. He came over, pasta machine in hand and flour and eggs in the other. He had a big smile and an open heart. He did not overthink things, instead he just lived in, whatever it was that he was doing in that particular moment. We started by creating a flour volcano on the table. I had to crack the eggs into the centre and then slowly combine the two ingredients. We then alternatingly proceeded to knead this dough for a solid twenty minutes, if not more. He wanted it to be perfectly firm. Springy. We then pushed it through the pasta machine, folding it again and again, pushing it back through, leaving us with long sheets of pasta. We let it set. We made love. He was good in bed and touched me in all the right places. The sheets of pasta now had to go back through the machine, but into pappardelle strips.

The sauce was a whole separate process. Point being: it took long. And usually I rush things. I count down the clock in whatever I do and I don't know why I do that. I don't know what I am counting towards or working towards, as I don't even know what my goals are in life. Usually it was counting down until I would be back home. That can't be it anymore. I tried to rush the pasta and Alberto kept coming over to me and slowing me down.

"Stop," he would say and kiss me. "Enjoy the process. Do it with love." I mocked it in my head. *Hah. 'Do it with love'*. But I knew that I had a lot that I needed to learn from him. About time, about passion and about thinking.

For years I fled through love without an orgasm, without true desire. I once made a list of all the guys I had ever kissed so that I could track the way I had evolved. Starting with absolutely nothing at high school, which may be why I still feel surprised every time a guy does reciprocate any of my tentative advances. Then my first boyfriend, a romantic, careful teenage entanglement, which when ended led to three years of university flirtation and fabulous flings. There are one or two boys on that kiss list that claimed to be deeply and truly in love with me, that fought for me over years and that followed me to whichever place I was in the world. It's difficult to describe how I felt in those instances. I was usually infatuated with another one by that point; usually guys that had no interest in any relationship whatsoever. I was truly and honestly wanted by good, intelligent guys and I could not give myself to them. I played with the idea and often attempted to push myself a little; to go on another date just to see if maybe this time I would feel something. But I didn't and I never pushed myself to enter a loveless relationship. Which I am proud of.

There was once a guy who seemed to tick all the arbitrary boxes and I went along with the charade, going on dates, going for drinks all the while knowing, but not admitting to myself, that I was not feeling anything that would resemble love. He invited me to his country home and once there, away from everything and everyone, the gravity of my mistake became so obviously constricting. I had never felt so claustrophobic as in his unquestioned life. Once I finally escaped and, alone again, I went through a wave of appreciation for myself. I couldn't believe how lucky I was to have myself, my mind, my family, my life at home, my questions: all of it. I did everything with a deep contentedness for the next few weeks. Not questioning being single but relishing my independence.

I told my therapist that I was trying out some dating apps and that I was scared of what people would think. "You are scared of so many things. Why?" he asked me. "I don't know why I am", I replied. "I think I just want to do things right." "You want to be liked," he said. "I suppose I do", admitting that, not pretending that I did not agree was already a great step for me. Admitting that not everything is perfect, that I fear so much, that I do embarrassing things and want things that I don't have. I used to be incapable of openly admitting such things. To say: 'I met this guy online, I was incapable of meeting someone normally.'

I had met Alberto online and he was different from other guys I had dated. Like I said earlier, I quickly realised that I had a lot to learn from him. About *time*, about *passion* and about *thinking*. That evening, when we made pasta, I kept on analysing him and thinking about the future, about what a future could look like together. Analysing his every move, if he was doing everything right, how my friends and my family would find him. He passed most of the tests with his smile. He stopped my train of thoughts every now and then, pulling myself towards him, passionately making love to me. For the first time helping me explore my body with me. Inexperienced and naïve, I had not done so myself. At the start of us, I felt inadequate in bed with him. But I tried to let go and to give myself to him and to what felt right in the moment. I would close my eyes and worry and then tell myself not to. I would stuff the pasta dough into the machine and then tell myself to relax and wait. This was the beginning of a journey of learning for me. Not learning about efficiency or social constructions or anthropological perspectives: this was learning about passion, time and how the two go together. About letting go. Appreciating my thoughts but not letting them take away from my life and the present. About becoming more sexually aware, appreciating our bodies as passionate pleasurable organisms that do not need to check boxes to feel fulfilled.

Chapter Seven

I come home to a parcel hidden behind the potted flowers on my doorstep. My heart jumps. There is also a postcard, layers of blue and yellow forming a cloud-like or possibly oceanic landscape. Quite striking, I think. I find the colour mysterious. It reminds me of the time of day known as 'gloaming'. The parcel has a beautiful papier mâché box with wrapped chocolate honeycomb pieces inside. I tried to make honeycomb a few times and it's not that difficult, but it's getting it just right with the honey and the sugar. You brown the sugar just enough. Because if you don't brown it enough, it gets too wet. When you do brown it, it gets a bit bitter. Then you add the baking powder and it turns into a frothy mess. After you take it off the heat and it cools, you have to bash it up around the place, to get those fine delicious flaky crispy bits. It's an art to get the right shade of brown. It has to be honey looking, inviting, delicious. And this one is. I turn over the postcard and in blue ink Arthur quotes Oscar Wilde and writes:

To live is the rarest thing in the world. Most people exist, that is all.

I'm looking forward to tomorrow. Arthur

I skim it quickly at first, searching for some deeper meaning and then slowly re-read the note three times before writing a note back. A text message may not be the same as a letter, but in this moment its immediacy trumps the beauty of a handwritten missive.

Dear Arthur,

I just came back to my flat and found this beautiful surprise on my doorstep! Someone you sent must have left it there. Thank you for being so thoughtful. The chocolate is delicious – I already had some of the honeycomb bits on the top!

And thank you for the box. It's beautiful. Where is it from? I love the colours and the texture. I will think of something lovely to put in it.

And, of course, most importantly, thank you for Wilde's wisdom. I have put it up on my wall already.

Love, Clara

He replies quickly.

Dear Clara,

Good evening from Dorset! I'm so glad it made its way to you intact. I had to remind my friend not to forget. My worst nightmare was that it would be left in my kitchen to melt for weeks. Left in limbo.

I had a feeling you may have a soft spot for sweet things. I go to the local deli for one thing and always get distracted by sauces, pestos or exotic pastas. I feel like every time

I go back, there's some new pasta with a new name, looking more delicious than the last.

I'm flattered you've pinned up the post-card. Now I have dedicated wall space in your apartment! I'm curious, where do you think the box is from? I don't know if those are your colours though.

I was just requisitioned by Fernanda to help with the watering of the garden. I never noticed quite how many pots there are until you need to water them all. There is something satisfying about giving plants a good drink in the evening after a hot day. The garden looks beautiful, you'll love it.

The evening sunlight is shining through the atelier windows just now and I'm feeling very inspired. I think I might have a hot, hot bath now and then work through the night...

Love, Arthur

I feel honoured that he took the time to do this for me. It makes me wonder: if someone feels inclined to perform such an act of kindness for my benefit, why am I so harsh on myself?

Chapter Eight

Growing up I would spend my summers in Spain, biking around the country roads behind our Finca. I vividly remember the rushing wind swirling around my face, blowing, billowing, brushing against my cheeks and bristling through my hair. I would wear headphones and listen to music that was impossible to hear over the wind. But, if I turned my face to the side, the music would ring loud and clearly in my ears. Facing forward, eyes on the road ahead, the tunes would be inaudible. Stopping to enjoy the view, to take a look around, letting my lungs inflate. Stopping. Turning away from the cemented path laid out by our society and pausing. That's what revealed the music to me. But it was dangerous. The country roads were curvy and rocky and the wheels of our bikes could easily slip. Cars would shoot around a blind spot, as though they were alone in this world. The rush of speed on a hill or the power of a song would oftentimes trump my fundamental sense of protection. And here I was thinking that natural selection protects our instinct for safety.

I prop Arthur's card on a pile of unread books and eventually start getting dressed for my second outing of the day. Exchanging the ballerinas for a pair of trainers and the jumper for a sweater that I got from my brother, I am ready in a minute or two. I push my Brompton bike out of the flat, crashing against corners, and step outside. It's drizzly now. I start treading, carefully stopping to observe and pre-empt any possible collisions. Fleeting past the housing estates just off Elizabeth Bridge and on the edge of Pimlico, I look up into all the tiny little yellow squares of light piling up on top of each other.

A few years ago, I flew to Corsica over Nice. I had never been to Nice or St Tropez, but I had heard about it. From my little plane window, I could see the towering apartment buildings crowding the airport surroundings. Once on the ground, I saw people wearing Gucci, smelling of Dior, and carrying Chanel, and all piling into Chelsea G-Wagons, one after the other. Flocking to St Tropez, but driving through the outskirts to get there. Although different here, I think of the sensation of randomness that I felt then. The borders and boundaries arbitrarily drawn throughout our world. The purest form of luck that determined in which home or country we were born. The complete lack of action from our side, in determining which nationality we got, and the deepest forms of entitlement towards people from another, continues to strike me every time I land on a border, if that be the Elizabeth Bridge or the Cote d'Azur.

I whiz through Hyde Park and Regent's Park, heading towards Camden. *Dining with the Tories and thinking with the Liberals.* Wilde's words go through my head as I think of the weekend ahead and my destination tonight. Where is the border there? Do I have one? Do I need one? Can I have one foot on either side? The migrants that I teach English can't, so why should I be able to?

*

"My son said he wants to kill himself," Fahima says matter of factly. I'd locked my bike outside the coldly lit Camden English Club: a spare room in a barely used community centre. My mother had forwarded the call for volunteers to lead a weekly evening English lesson a few months ago and I applied on a whim, thinking an unqualified dual citizen would not quite meet the criteria. I started the week after.

"Jayden said that?" I look at Fahima's confused, pained face. She is one of five women who come every week. Every now and then a stray participant joins for a session or two, but these five women are always here. We start each lesson by telling each other something that has happened this week. Everyone has to ask at least one question and the person sharing has to answer in full sentences. Fahima had illegally come to London from Somalia with her youngest son Jayden, when she was thirty. After an endless and impossibly difficult process, they finally gained permanent settled status. But their journey traumatized her. The memories of sex payments for bus fares or boots for Jayden tormented her. The crossing of the border broke her. Jayden was submitted into the foster care system after Fahima had been found high on crack with him for the third time in front of their council estate. She needed the artificial escape from her reality.

I have never used drugs, but the thought is enticing. The idea of expanding our horizons by using a cocktail of ingredients to push away the constricting insecurities and limits of our minds, is a relevant one. The danger of becoming addicted to this new version of reality is a dangerous one. I was riding my bike out of Victoria Station recently, closing my nose as I passed through the gathering of smokers that forms beyond the ticket barriers every day. It struck me how many people breathe in smoke, knowing that it destroys their chances of living a longer, healthier life. The concept of addiction and control hit me: how much control do we actually have over our lives and over what we want? If so, many people willingly submit themselves to a short life for the very acquired taste of smoke in their lungs, then what else do we do, all the while, knowing it may not be the best for us?

"He said it in class and his teacher overheard him. The other boys told her that he is getting beaten at home."

"Beaten by whom? By the foster family?" I ask.

"Hah. If you can call it a family. It's a middle-aged woman and her sister."

"Fahima, is there anything that we can do? Can't you get involved?"

"Nothing...I can't believe it...it's all my fault...I...I...This is Jayden. And he wants to die." Her face is empty and the greyish bags under her eyes sink into her cheekbones. Fahima is allowed to see Jayden four times a year. Until she can prove that she has been sober for more than a year, they will not start building a case for her. She is coming here to learn English so that, when the day comes where she will have to stand up and fight for custody, she will be able to articulate her thoughts into clear sentences.

"We have been working so hard." Lena speaks softly. She is a delicate Polish lady who works as a cleaner for a family in Kensington. She puts her hand on Fahima's shoulder. "I think you should go and talk to the social services."

"First let us remember that Jayden is ten. Death is a difficult notion for a young child to understand. The ending of our life must seem like a brief escape from his struggles. Not permanent," I say.

"Do you really think so?" Fahima whispers.

"I do. I don't think that it's possible for a kid to understand what death actually means. I mean, I hardly do."

"It is very simple. When you die, you go to Heaven or you go to Hell," Rosemarie speaks confidently. "Everyone knows that."

I dig my feet into the soft but stubborn insoles that I had made to perfectly shape and direct my walk and posture. Fahima is sitting, shoulders slumped next to me, head in her hands. I touch her, holding the palm of my hand to her back. Slowly brushing backwards and forwards, showing her that I am here next to her, supporting her from a distance, across a border.

"Do you believe?" Rosemarie takes my silence as defiance.

"In what?" I ask, knowing what it is she wants to know. Religion and belief have become the same thing over the years.

She holds her hands up in the air, presumably pointing to the elderly invisible man that she calls God. "Religious world views are all subjective. Pascal believed that God is in our heart, not in our rational mind", I say.

"So, you don't believe in God?" she asks. "I do. I think he is true with my rational mind."

"I don't think that you can rationally explain religion, it is a belief, like you said, Rosemarie. Pascal was a physicist, but the more he dived into physics the more he realized how much is left unexplained by the laws of physics. At some point he became a philosopher of religion. The benefits of believing were so great for him, that despite being unlikely to be true, he betted on God's existence. He believed that there has to be a higher power to explain that which we cannot explain."

"God *can* explain everything," insists Rosemarie. "There is a reason for everything. There is a reason why Jayden said that he wants to kill himself."

"How can there be a reason for a young boy wanting to kill himself? I believe. But I also question most of what I believe in."

"Some things are not meant to be questioned. He is punishing me," Fahima rebukes. "I failed Him and I am so sorry."

"You did not fail anyone, Fahima," I tell her. "You were born into a very specific set of circumstances that made your life specifically difficult for you as a person."

"What are you talking about Clara!?" she pleads.

"I'm just trying to say that we cannot be accountable for everything that happens in our lives. Biology and chemistry follow rules and some may argue that our personalities are formed by these complex systems, one thing leading to another. A cause and effect. If everything were logically sequenced, there would be no freedom of will. That would mean you did not actually choose to make the mistakes that you did."

"But that would mean everyone is always off the hook for whatever they do!" Milika, a chirpy Afghan girl, adds.

"Yeah, I guess you're right. I mean there are paradoxes which you cannot solve, no matter how long you think about it. Which proves the opposite: that life isn't all pre-determined."

"All I know is I fear for Jayden. God or no God, I played a role in the way he's feeling right now and I feel guilty," says Fahima.

"I think that the best that you can do right now is just hope that his foster mother is not actually beating him and that he did not mean what he said," I offer.

"Hope is uncertainty and uncertainty has no place in believers. Have faith, Fahima," Rosemarie persists.

Fahima shuffles forward and whispers as though she were telling us a very deep secret. "It is so difficult for me to see clearly right now. Of course, I want what is best for my son, but I really struggle with wishing this lady well. I once heard a question that asked: 'If you had the option to get 200,000 pounds for free but that would mean that your biggest enemy automatically gets 2,000,000 pounds for free, would you take the 200,000 pounds?'. My initial reaction was: 'of course I would take it!' But it is harder than you think to watch a person you dislike or are in competition with, have what you can't have."

"Jayden is not like money. She has Jaden for now and you need to do everything you can to hope that they are happy, for his good." I muster with all my strength, struggling with the complexity of her emotions and her position. "You *will* get him back."

I always used to believe that emotions (sadness, anxiety) were contextual and that their subjective nature in each individual context equalised the experience of pain in the world. You always hear those stories of children in Africa smiling, despite their existential problems and the Western rich getting more depressed each year. But now, as I ride my bike across the bridge, I can't help but think that the sadness and confusion and struggle that I feel is embedded in a sense of security and safety that none of these women have. It is luck, I guess, randomness that I was born on the right side of the border, into a geographical safety net.

I study the council houses fly past me, slowly beginning to give way to the white homes of Chelsea. From an architectural perspective, you only have to look at the difference between 18th century and 19th century British architecture to understand most of Victorian adventurism and grandeur. If you go to Fitzroy square in Fitzrovia you see a Robert Adam plain, formal, grand square but nothing ostentatious. But if you take a little trip down South Kensington and look at the monumental and powerful Natural History Museum, it flaunts the classical heritage.

The Victorians thought that they could conquer the entire world and built an infrastructure that reflected just that. The London sewers created after The Great Stink in 1858 were designed for months by the Victorians. Some of the finest wrought iron works, columns and capitals were designed and manufactured. Nobody would ever see them apart from the workers painting them initially. The ideal that the Victorians had influenced their opinion on people that were less developed. Certainly, from a racial perspective, but also a triumphal perspective: they were going to rule the world.

When you study how and why some nations developed, you can look at the psychology of the people at the time. We need to have proxies for their psychology to understand what they were thinking about the world around them. Looking at Chinese maps: from the 16th century you notice that on the piece of paper the map of their known world covers the entire map. There are no blank spaces. It is as if the Chinese felt that they knew all they needed to know and, beyond this realm, there was nothing more for them to discover or understand. Whereas European maps have large blank spaces, wondering what is in those spaces that we don't know, what they could explore.

Chapter Nine

I am standing on the soft, pale green grass lining the cliffs. Beneath me, the raging waves crunch against stone. I let my mind wonder to an unknown place. I imagine myself curling into the rough slabs of water. What would it feel like to let go of the tight grasp that life has on us? To simply give up?

I stand on this majestic pedestal of nature, overlooking one of nature's wildest, most uncontrollable elements. The different shades of darkness twist and intertwine into deep pools. I pluck a blade of grass from the padded cushion of mingling greens beneath me. My grandfather taught me what to do next. I use my outgrown nails to cut a little strip in the middle of the piece of grass and press the opening against my creased lips. The slightest sound escapes from my construction. It is inaudible. I compete with the loud waves, blowing harder, pushing more air through the plucked grass. The sound that I create echoes softly in my own vicinity but remains just another forgotten tone in the loudness surrounding me.

I cry out and scream. My lungs burn and my eyes water from the cold air thrashing around me. Images flash through my mind. Memories bounce off one another, one triggering moment seeping into another. An incredible contradiction of lightness and darkness is taking place in my mind and it is out of control. My mind is out of my control and yet it is mine. There are things that we can control and things that are out of our reach; aspects of life that belong to a higher power. My mind is running loose. Like it always has. So, I take control of what I can:

my body. A step forward and my life would end. I mull this over, as though it were an option, all the while knowing that it is not. I imagine what my body would look like down there. I conjure up the reactions of Arthur, my friends and my acquaintances. I play with the idea, enjoying the fact that I could at any moment make this a reality.

The fact, however, remains that it is just an idea. I understand the beauty of life but let myself forget from time to time. The messiness of life is better than no life at all. Once gone, all is gone. Pain is better than no sensation at all. Messiness is interesting but emptiness is nothing at all. The psychological barrier that prevents us from making this figment a reality is indescribably strong. Our mind controls our body and what we do. But what controls our mind? Our soul?

Two heads bob up and down at the far end of the path. Anger reveals itself inside me, at the sight of this intrusion. The distant figures laugh as they climb over the stile and help one another. The elderly man goes first and grips the woman's hand tightly, as she balances her body weight over the wooden beams. Happiness is linked to other people. A collective consciousness cradles beings.

Life is circumstantial. That is something we often forget. There are different sets of different problems that always influence people. We live in a bubble, embedded in our surroundings, the things that we know, the people that we know, the aspirations that the people we know aspire towards. I turn my back to whatever it was that I was doing and make my way home.

Chapter Ten

I am off to Dorset. A day earlier than the boys. Promising that I won't be a nuisance to his art making, I drive out bringing books and distractions. It is very dark outside, and the drive is beautiful. I've taken my father's car for the next few days. He had bought a Jaguar convertible in his late thirties, but only after giving in to my mother's condition to give away double the amount to charity. After a few spins it had ended up in the garage, barely used.

My belly is swirling with anxious butterflies, tumbling around in the back of my throat all the way down to my gut. Bouncing off of each other, they are subtly choking me with fear. Whatever it is that I am doing, they are there to remind me of what is ahead. It's interesting how we fear certain things and live through other events with pure ease. Human connection is what brings us the greatest joy, but also what petrifies us most. Because we mostly feel that we have something to lose. What we forget is that most people think this way and so are focused on themselves and what they believe they have to lose, instead of studying our own minute behaviour. And yet, knowing this, I feel fear for something relatively mundane, drawing out possible awkward or devastatingly embarrassing conclusions.

Usually I end up cleaning out my closet or spring cleaning my flat for the hundredth time to distract myself. Now with my eyes on the road, I have to submit to the butterflies, knowing that this is it. There is no turning back, no more decision making: I am going to be spending a weekend with a man who I do not know well at all. I try to focus every part of my brain that I can still control on the surroundings gliding past me, looking at each tree and field with magnifying eyes. Going west is always an amazing drive in the evening, because you're chasing the sun over the horizon. Listening to music, looking at the different types of clouds in the sky. I have never seen so many different combinations. It's an amazing place and lies at the very heart of the concept of England. As someone born in London but with German roots, I feel a kinship with England, a country forged by ancient Germanic tribes. There are such deep and abiding ties between England and Germany, but they have largely been forgotten thanks to the events of the last century.

I arrive at Arthur's cottage. Yellow light glows out of the windows and in the evening musk it looks like a refuge that any wandering soul would want to enter. I stop the car in the gravel driveway and close my eyes. I deeply breathe in the earthy, fresh night air. My lungs expand and wonder why we usually breathe so shortly. I do a small ritual that I often do in times of stress. By creating mental checkboxes, I comb through my life and check off elements in the hope that it will give me a sense of peace.

Family: I have met my mother for lunch this week and am in contact with my siblings, checking up that they are happy and doing well. Check. Friends: I have been partaking in the social agenda of London. Check. Work: apart from the odd freelance article, this remains a question mark, a mystery. What to do with my life and my questions and my purpose seems impossible for me to know at this point. I shake my head at myself, marveling at the fact that I still do this ritual so often. Marveling at the fact that it provides me with a sense of peace, when all it entails is going through society's expectations for myself.

I find myself thinking about how these expectations shape us. If I wanted to, I could mould my existence, like a small lump of clay, into whatever wild, primal, passionate shape I desire. And yet I find myself hardening into a sculpture that has been modelled by a power quite unknown to me. Modern life provides the water with which I might soften this form, and yet I cannot seem to find the strength.

*

Labels:
hiding under the cover
of a
superficial
veil.

So easy and obvious
to expose.

But never done.

Why destroy
the game of charades
that everybody seems to enjoy
that everybody seems so invested in.

What would happen
if out of curiosity

the numbers
the names
the hierarchies
the places

the expectations
the milestones
the reputations
the borders
the cultures
the sexes

had no meaning.

That judgement
had no place
because there was nothing
left to judge.

That we float free of perception
of fear
of self-fulfilling prophecies

and return our artificial constructions of selves
to the council

exchanging them for
the raw
the unleashed
the found
the intrinsic
unconstructed
me.

*

Arthur walks towards me, not from the house, but from a path leading somewhere that I can't quite make out in the darkness. He is smiling widely, wearing baggy jeans and a loose-fitting white linen shirt.

"What are you doing hiding away in your car?" he asks. "I heard you come in a while ago."

"I know, I know," I reply, a little embarrassed. "I was distracted by my own thoughts."

"Aren't we all? Come in, come in. Lots of time for day, or night, dreaming out here."

He opens the back of the Jaguar and takes out my weekend bag. We crunch over the gravel and through the arched wooden door. It smells of freshly baked bread and mint. Cold slabs of stone line the hallway. Large and small antlers hang on every corner, parading successful hunting trophies. Arthur takes me up the stairs to my room. The wallpaper is a deep green, with a faint pattern of gold leaf. The bed matches this arrangement almost with the gold leaf instead shining on a background of burgundy. Thick white pillows are tucked under the duvet. Thin wooden nightstands on both sides of the bed are covered in lamps, candles, and little plates for jewelry.

"Why don't you take a moment to unpack and I'll get a bottle of red for us to drink. Just come down to the living room. Bottom of the stairs on your left."

I leave my bags on the floor and drop myself onto the bed. I feel sleep coming quickly and so force myself up and splash cold water over my face in the adjacent bathroom. I take my blazer and boots off and, leaving the jeans and white blouse on, slip into some navy ballerinas.

The walls in the living room are red and large paintings in heavy gold frames hang on either side of the room. A red Moroccan rug flags the floor. Two large, dark, antique armoires are pushed against the walls and are scattered with photo frames. Arthur is comfortably settled in the matching patterned cream and red upholstered sofa.

The room moves into an alcove, home to a large black grand piano and opens up to French doors, leading to a dining room around the corner. Now, up close, I see Arthur's trousers and shirt are full of clay. He has a three-day beard growing with snippets of dried paint lodged into some of the creases. His longer hair is pushed back behind his ears and he looks at ease.

"I'm so glad you're here, and that you came before the others arrive. I was very productive today, trying to push forward so we would have a little more time together."

"Can you force art to come to you faster?"

"With the right incentives, maybe..." He laughs. "I'm just joking. I had planned to be ready for when the chaps come on Friday, so really, I was just adding the finishing touches."

"Can I see?"

"Ahh...we'll have to see about that."

"But I haven't seen any of your work yet. Neither in Notting Hill and not here. Where is it all stashed?!"

"My work doesn't leave the atelier unless it goes to buyers."

"You're really something."

"Oh, I'm certainly something," he teases. I can tell that he has done this before and fear settles into my belly. I was wrong. It is not me who will lose interest. I know this in that second. I wonder if it is precisely this shift in thought that changes my behaviour and their response to my suddenly pressing urgency in emotion. This is not him being easy, this is him relaxing into the role of an admired artist. A bachelor reaping the benefits of his desirability.

In my split second of indecision, he leans forward and presses his lips against mine. I indulge myself in the mingling of our bodies, pushing away my rising fears.

*

A tugging
Kampf
between the
monstrous mind
and the
forgiving heart.

The heart
usually wins,
anticipating
the loss ahead.

Chapter Eleven

I awake already hungover from the three bottles of wine last night. After hours of exhilarating conversation, my mind for once right there, in that moment Arthur, the supposed gentleman that he is, had walked me up to my room and sent me to bed with a lasting kiss. Too tired to contemplate what its meaning was, I fell into a dreamless sleep.

I open up my window and look out into a sea of green. Layer upon layer of trees and fabulously singing birds dot the view. I cannot take my eyes off the strip of ocean, in the far distance. A cinnabar moth has just flown into my room. The smell of coffee and strawberries lures me downstairs. I brush my teeth, wash my face and apply a trace of makeup. Wearing a matching cream skirt and blouse set and ballerinas, I hop down the stairs.

Fernanda is Brazilian and beautiful. Covered in smiles and radiance, she bustles around the kitchen, working on all sorts of concoctions. The contents of Arthur's Notting Hill fridge now make much more sense. He is sitting at the table and looks up from the newspaper, croissant in hand. I am not quite sure what is applicable at this moment in time: a hug, or a kiss, or nothing at all. He makes the decision for me, by giving me half of a wave and staying firmly seated at the table.

"Good morning! I hope you slept well." His voice is kind, even if his greeting lacks any accompanying action.

"I did. I could hear the birds chirping this morning and spent so long just looking out of the window. It was beautiful."

"The view was better when I was little, but now that the trees have grown the Somerset Levels are harder to see. The flowers should be out in the meadows by now. Why don't you go for a wander on the farm?"

"We went to a local yoghurt maker a few days ago," Fernanda chimes in. "They have a vending machine system in the local towns where people go and fill their own glass bottles from a cooled vat of fresh milk. Do you want to try some?"

"Why not?" I reply. "Usually I stick to oat milk, or almond, because of all the scare stories about dairy milk being pumped full of hormones."

"This is definitely free of all that nonsense," she assures me, shaking her head at my urban worries.

Over milky coffee and delicious fruit bowls, we lightly enjoy each other's company.

"So, what is there to do around here?" I ask Arthur.

"Well, I've always spent summers here walking on Cadbury Castle, checking out the neighbours' bees, shooting in the woods, picking wild garlic and mushrooms, some very competitive games of croquet and fishing on the Avon...the list goes on and on! This is paradise."

"I'd love to see your atelier..."

"Give me a little more time to curve around some finishing touches and then I'll take you. Deal?"

He stands to leave and almost comically takes my hand to kiss it. But before his lips touch my skin, he studies it, uncurling one finger at a time.

Left slightly perplexed, I step out of the kitchen onto a wood-panelled terrace and properly see the house for the first time in daylight. The house is two parts. One side is old brick with rustic wooden framed windows. The glass has diamond-shaped panes and the roof is slightly

dented and crooked. There are little subsections and layered protruding rooms and balconies. The windows are
all different shapes: some are large, rounded, arched windows and some are small peak holes. Wooden beams cut
through the old brick and an old chimney takes up half of
the roof. And then it pushes back into a light, huge modern wooden barn-like extension. That must be the atelier.
The two parts merge together, with bundles of ivory and
white roses that twist and turn over the whole exterior. It
is as though the house extends the garden, which has been
beautifully designed. A finely mown croquet lawn to the
back and a whimsical sea of purple lavender, beige hay
and blue daffodils spread across the front. A boat house
with green shutters is at the far side of a small overgrown
lily-pad filled lake. It is truly what I would call paradise.

*

Later, I am sitting on a bench staring into the abyss of
merging greens and yellows. I have two books with me.
I have that, which I will start reading, *Letters to a Young
Poet* by Rilke, and I have a small introduction to art history, only about one hundred pages, giving a whistle stop
tour of everything from Renaissance art to the famed Mr.
Pollock so that I don't completely embarrass myself in
front of Arthur.

After breakfast, I went for a run through the local
parks and down to the village and back up through lovely
deer parkland. It is a fantastic forest, except the hill is
hellishly steep. I totally fell for the sales pitch about lightness and stiffness and bought new 'marathon' running
shoes. You go down a rabbit hole of gear that you can
buy to enhance your running, but the biggest thing that
you can do is just learning how to control your breath.

The worst ones are the gentle slopes. Everyone can do a short uphill power through for five minutes, but it's that slow gentle rise that just keeps on going where I get knackered. I have learnt that I can run much harder and for much longer when I control my breath. Four breaths in and four breaths out. It is very easy to start compromising on the in-breaths, which supply the muscles with oxygen. The out-breaths are of course much easier. Focusing on managing the in-breaths and making sure I get a big gulp of air distracts me and the time goes very quickly, especially if you have a good stream of songs.

It is very quiet when I make my way back down to the cottage. So quiet that I can hear my own breathing and feet pressing down on the gravel. Serene. I tentatively walk towards the huge glass doors of the barn. Standing outside I can see Arthur working. The thick walls dampen thunderous music which escapes from the sound system. I feel like I am invading a very personal moment. He is pressing his hands against a piece of clay, moulding, shaping a figure. His face is scrunched up in deep concentration. His hands are steady. It is in that moment that I feel drawn to his soul. The work that he is doing is raw and honest, something very rare nowadays. I feel he almost accumulates intuition with all of the layers of knowledge built in his mind into a projection of the reality that he sees around him.

I release my eyes from their fixation and let them wonder around the atelier. Flooded with the golden afternoon light through ten great glass dome-shaped windows, the barn becomes a beacon of brilliance. A far brick wall is covered in sketches. Empty canvases are piled in one corner. Next to them is a large table with rows upon rows of materials, clay, acrylic paint, brushes and shaping tools.

The polished concrete floor is home to a myriad of sculptures. I have never seen raw beauty in such an honest form. Small, tiny, curvaceous, bony, dark or pale figures of all beautifully crafted women dot the place. Some so opposed to anything that we dictate as beautiful, that you have to stop and ask yourself why you find it so intrinsically wonderful. I am reminded of the little figure that I saw that one weekend in Paris and I feel as though something is connecting at this moment in time. As though, for the first time, something was meant to be. I put my hand over my heart and feel it beating. I feel it pumping blood and I feel my body work, keeping me alive. And I whisper, 'thank you'. For the first time in a very long while, I feel at home in the shell that I have been given. What a precious privilege it is to be alive.

Arthur feels my presence and turns around. His hair is held back with a headband and he has a clay tool stuck behind his ear. We just look at each other through the window for a moment and he cocks his head and smiles. Wearing a white linen shirt covered in clay he walks towards me and opens the glass door.

"Close your eyes," he says, and takes my hand in his. I can feel the coarse calluses of a sculptor press against my soft palms. He turns the music off and I let him lead me through the darkness of the atelier. He touches my hand to a cool, hard, slightly wet surface.

"This is the last sculpture I have to finish," he says. "I want you to feel the figure and tell me what you think."

I oblige, and let my fingers trace the soft curves of a female body. My fingers reach the middle of the chest and come to a stop over the left breastbone. I breathe sharply and my closed eyes begin to water.

"It's beautiful and soft and…"

"It is you."

I open my eyes and see that his are wide with antici-
pation.

"I'm sorry if this is overstepping the mark. I started
working on this on Tuesday, and before I knew it, my
hands were recreating the woman that was on my mind."

Unsure of what he is saying, I begin to wonder how
many women he has on his mind, and whether they are
always memorialised in sculptures. Undeterred, I reach
up and kiss him.

Chapter Twelve

Only a few moments later, we hear Richard, George and Hugo arrive. They are laughing, and at least one of them is already slightly tipsy, when they charge into the atelier and envelop us in a hug.

"Agh! It feels great to be out here," says George. Or maybe Hugo. In the mêlée it is difficult to tell.

"I'm so happy you guys made it safely," says Arthur. "Looks like you have already had a beer or two!"

"Or ten!" exclaims Hugo. "And we brought enough wine to get the Cerne Abbas Giant plastered."

"Thanks so much for inviting us, Arthur," says George. "It's beautiful as always."

The trance that Arthur and I were in, is well and truly broken. In its place, an easy air of relaxed jokes and familiar faces.

The smell of roasting food draws us to the front terrace. I am careful not to step onto the cracks between the stones. What laughter must our superstitions provide to fate, I think. I don't truly think that we are important enough to have someone watching over us at all times and punishing us for stepping on a crack or not throwing salt over our shoulders. And yet I do it. Just to be sure. Because what were the chances that I exist and that my life turned out the way that it did?

Fernanda has prepared an array of potato salads, dips, lamb's lettuce and grilled vegetables on the wooden table overlooking the lake. It is a mild evening; the sun is glistening golden in our faces, and we comfortably settle into conversation. Arthur comes out carrying a wooden board of marinated steaks and sausages, ready to throw on the grill. Soft chilled music is playing in the background and that distinct smell of grill smoke – that when wafting over a garden in the city will make you dream of summer – fills the air. Over loud conversation and exchange of views, I catch Arthur looking at me and we lock eyes.

"I say," asks Richard, "is there a hospital anywhere near this backwater of yours?"

"Funnily enough there is," Arthur replies. "There's also running water, electricity, and even the internet."

"What are you asking about hospitals for?" enquires George.

"Well, before I offended our gracious host, I was going to say I think I might fall into a food coma from this wonderful repast we're enjoying."

"Don't worry," Arthur assures him, "you can walk off your overindulgence tomorrow and give me some peace to get back to work."

"My dear Arthur, there aren't enough steps between here and Hell to let me walk off my overindulgence."

"Isn't that exactly what doctors are trying to do nowadays?" asks Hugo. "Instead of doling out medicine they're prescribing exercise. A friend of mine was actually given an Apple Watch by her doctor on the condition that she walks 10,000 steps per day. The watch actually records her movements, and if she doesn't meet her targets it will be taken away from her."

"I'd much rather have a priest demand I say 10,000 'Hail Mary's than a doctor demand I take 10,000 steps a day. How ghastly."

Ignoring Richard's *bon mot*, Arthur returns to the subject at hand. "I take it your friend has private health insurance. I can't see the NHS giving out Apple Watches."

"You'd be lucky to be given an actual *apple* by the NHS nowadays," jokes Richard. "It's a total disaster."

"Oh come off it, Richard. When was the last time you used the NHS?" Hugo isn't angry, but he's had enough drink that his retort comes off more pointed than it was perhaps intended to. "Anyway, it's impossible to make sweeping statements about the NHS as it's become so atomised. Everything depends on where you are in the country, the so-called 'postcode lottery'. It also depends on factors such as social class, age, and how acute your condition is."

"Of course," George agrees. "We all happen to live near good hospitals. If you get sick and you go to the Chelsea and Westminster, you're going to get good treatment."

"Yes," continues Hugo. "But if you end up in a hospital on the outskirts of Middlesbrough, your experience will be very different."

"Isn't that true, no matter where in the world you are?" I ask. "Even in the most utopian healthcare systems, your experience is going to be affected by social factors, and regional differences. Not least because the wealthier you are, the better your health tends to be."

"You're right, Clara," says Hugo. "But in a system, that's supposed to be free at the point of use, it shouldn't matter what your status is. The quality of care should be the same, and it should be capable of balancing out such discrepancies."

"That's a wonderful ideal, but that's all it is. An ideal." Now that Arthur has finally decided to join the debate, I feel transfixed, fascinated to hear his perspective.

"It may be an ideal, but the NHS was founded on that ideal, and should be better placed to make that ideal a reality than any other system. What better system is there?"

"Well," says Arthur. "I actually think insurance shouldn't be seen as the preserve of the wealthy but should be more available to the entire population, for the benefit of everyone. I have private insurance, right, and my taxes help pay for the NHS. Now, that's not a bad thing because I can afford it, I don't mind my taxes helping others, but I also know that, by going private, I can get a better level of care. But people who aren't so lucky pay more money in tax to help the NHS than they would need to pay to go private. In other words, if they didn't pay any taxes, they'd be able to afford a better level of care, but they can't because they're locked into a tax system that makes them reliant on the NHS."

"I think you're right," says Hugo. "At least inasmuch as taxation in this country doesn't work, or the way the government spends that money."

"It's like the Houses of Parliament themselves," suggests George. "From the outside, they look beautiful, but inside it's full of Victorian pipes and Edwardian wiring that are ready to blow at a moment's notice. When money isn't spent on the real problems, whether it's an old building or a healthcare system, anything you do will be purely cosmetic."

"So, the answer isn't to change the system of taxation," I offer, "but to change the system of spending, making the government more accountable for where and why public money is being spent."

"To be fair, there is some accountability," says George. "When I send HMRC my tax return, they send me back a pie chart explaining where my taxes get spent. Though I've never noticed a section saying 'money to Boris' friends'."

"There isn't a country on earth where you won't find the powers that be skimming something off the top. It doesn't mean there's anything wrong with the system. In finance, it's expected that people will dip their finger in the pot, so you work around it. At the end of the day, any economy needs banks, because they provide financing for investment, which supports businesses, which provides jobs, which creates tax revenues." By now, Richard is already halfway through a speech we have all heard him recite countless times before. "So, without banks, there would be no chance of social equality, because the tax revenues that are used to provide social services are ultimately dependent on, you guessed it, the banks."

"So, in a nutshell," teases Arthur, "you're saving us all!"

"Indeed I am. Raise a glass, everyone, to me and my ilk, the real saviours of society!"

The evening fades from gold to yellow, to black with glistening stars and a shining moon lighting our way back inside. Fernanda has lit a fire and, with mugs of peppermint tea in hand, we settle around the radiating heat, suddenly tired.

"I'll have a little drink of something and be out for the count," Hugo announces.

I step outside while the boys talk. I am overlooking the endless fields, now layers of shadows in the darkness. I am sated with good food, conversation, ideas, the natural world of wonders surrounding me and with time to reflect, to wonder, to dream, to grow. I breathe. In. And out. In. And out.

*

Do you feel that you have power? That you could do anything? Do you let yourself dream? Most people live a life that many have already lived before. The rarest people dare to push the boundaries of what this life has to offer. I feel free and open. Free from fear of the unknown and the pressures of the world. I let myself dream.

Arthur steps out to join me, smiling softly. He has shaved his beard as though marking some sort of completion in his work. Done, dusted and back in the civilized world of order and handsome rules. He stands next to me, our shoulders touching, and it reminds me of the first night that I met him.

"You're always thinking."

"I know. Aren't you?"

He laughs and puts his arms around me, turning me to face him. I search his face for a clue to his feelings; look as far into his eyes as I can to get some sort of indication as to what all of this means. But he just smiles an ambiguous smile that could mean countless things. I pull him towards me and kiss him slowly.

I pull away and look at him.

"Come with me," he says. Taking my hand, he leads me up to his bedroom, pushing me against the walls of his house, pressing himself against me, on to me.

"Let me in." He whispers into my ear and I kiss him harder. My hand finds his back and my nails dig into his soft skin. I kiss his neck, breathing in his fresh smell of the outside and fire and aftershave, all mingled with sweat. Opening the buttons of his white shirt, I push him back towards the opposite wall. His hands move quickly, tugging at my straps, pushing them down, almost ripping the front open to reach my soft cupped bra. His lips find my breasts, biting against the soft flesh.

"Up." He utters and carries me, so that my legs wrap around his waist. We only just manage to reach the top of the staircase, dropping things here and there, but not caring. Lost in the moment of desire, the pressing, touching, driving need for passion and release. My hands grip his hair, tugging his head backwards, pushing him away ever so slightly and then back towards me again. In bed, stripped and close, I let him kiss me and look up at the ceiling. I feel my mind beginning to wonder, going somewhere that will rip me out of this reverie, that will let my body go on but not me. As if he notices, Arthur puts his hands around my face and again, more forceful this time says: "Let me in."

I want to. I want to let him in and I try to. I bring my mind back and I flip Arthur around, so that I sit on top of him, slowly kissing and stopping. Kissing and stopping and holding his face. Kissing and stopping and running my hands down his chest. Kissing and stopping and tugging his hair, pushing his arms down and trying to give myself to him.

Chapter Thirteen

Mark arrives in the morning and, itchy from the ride, immediately asks to go out for a walk. So, off we go, with instruction from Fernanda to look for some wild herbs for her pesto sauce.

I have only met Mark once or twice over the years. He is Richard's identical twin and thus shares his features. A fiery temper makes up for a slightly smaller socially idealized height. The biggest difference between the two is probably Mark's more liberal outlook on life, in contrast to Richard' s very conservative, at times almost elitist, view on things. Both, however, share their humour and wit – it must have come from their parents.

"Have you noticed how the direction of the wind has changed?" asks Arthur, to no-one in particular. "A few days ago, it was still. A little bit windy, but it was a warm southwesterly wind. It's so much colder now. A northeastern wind, must be from the Arctic."

We're walking up from the house towards the Dorset Gap. The landscape is stunning.

Ignoring Arthur's murmurings, Mark exclaims: "Exciting news, our parents are getting a new puppy! I was already on the phone in bed this morning to the chap who runs The Dog House, where we used to send Bracken, our old lab."

"I had been campaigning for a golden retriever, to no avail," Richard begrudgingly admits. "The rest of the clan is very much in the Labrador camp."

"Poor Richard, things never go your way, do they?" teases Mark. "Well, the new pooch is a black lab, but we're in two minds about names. She's a she, so we're thinking either Baffin, although maybe that would make her sound a bit dim, or stroma."

"Can you imagine shouting 'Stroma' across a busy park?" asks Richard. "Christ, do we have to announce bourgeois quite so audibly?"

"What do you think, Clara?" Mark asks, earnestly.

"I agree with Richard."

"You do?!" exclaims Hugo, "That's rarely a good sign."

"What I meant," I continue, laughing, "is that, somewhere in Richard's typically snide comment, was a good point. Our attitudes towards dogs *do* reveal a lot about our class."

"Where are you going with this, Clara?" asks George.

"Hear me out. Firstly, all the breeds we have today came about because of the jobs we needed those dogs to do, right?"

"Right," the boys reply simultaneously. After days of listening to them share their manifestos, it's quite gratifying to command their undivided attention.

"And those jobs were determined largely by class. So, bloodhounds, setters, retrievers, all sorts of hunting dogs would largely have been the preserve of the wealthy. But herding dogs, collies for example, would have been kept by rural workers."

"Ok, good point," says Hugo.

"Secondly, while that may not be the case so much anymore, the fact remains that only the wealthiest people can afford the most expensive breeds, while the vast majority of people, who can't afford purebreds, are more likely to own some sort of mix, or cross, or even mongrels."

"Well I'm happy to return the favour and say that I entirely agree with Clara," says Richard. "But I'd go one further: there's not much difference between purebred dogs and the aristocracy. They're both the product of generations of incest and inbreeding, after all."

"What does our resident geneticist think?" asks George, as we turn to Hugo, expectantly.

"Well, once again Richard makes a good point despite himself. Genetically speaking, there's not that much difference between the problems some dogs experience thanks to their breeding and the illnesses or susceptibilities experienced by humans, who are the product of a shallow gene pool. Look at the Romanovs. It's no wonder *Haemophilia* was called 'the royal disease'."

"So, what you're saying is that, like mongrels, humans are better off when they mix as much as possible?" asks Mark.

"Don't tell the Brexiteers, folks, miscegenation is the future!" jokes George.

"What about twins?" asks Richard.

"Er, what about twins?" replies Hugo.

"Well, I take your point about inbreeding amongst humans contributing to genetic problems, but how do you account for profound differences between people who are genetically identical, such as Mark and myself?"

"Good question, brother!" exclaims Mark. "He's right, and it's not just our nature that was the same, our nurture was too."

"Well, I'd contest that," says Richard.

"Come on! The same family, the same school..."

"I'm afraid I don't have an immediate answer for you," says Hugo, after some moments of quiet contemplation. "There's actually a lot of evidence that suggests identical twins aren't all that identical. Genetically, yes, they are about as identical as two humans can be. But epigenetically, there is a whole host of factors that might vary, especially *in utero*: their position in the womb, the amount of oxygen they receive, the distribution of nutrients through the blood…"

"Well, the biggest difference between Richard and myself is that I'm gay and he, boring and square as he is about most things, is straight. Is that somehow down to epigenetics?"

"Possibly," says Hugo, "but it's impossible to establish a causal link. For the most part, sexuality is the product of nature and nurture in equal measure, so to speak. By which I mean most people are simply 'born this way', but they are also influenced by their experiences. That being said, it's likely that one day genetics might be able to pinpoint factors we simply can't see at the moment."

"So, there might really be such a thing as a 'gay gene'?" asks George.

"Not exactly, but we might be able to establish a link between sexuality and genetic predisposition. Look at this way, in studying genetic predisposition you have to sequence the genomes of loads and loads of people. Normally in families. So, you sequence the hell out of all the genes and look for potential changes in genes that could increase the risk of, for example, a disease. Take breast cancer, that's down to the BRCA mutation. If you've got a BRCA mutation, you're predisposed to breast cancer."

"That creates an increased risk of what, 15% or something?" I offer.

"Yes," says Hugo. "But you could have small changes in 30 different genes, each contributing to 0.005% increased risk. Individually, they might not mean much. But collectively, they give you a risk of maybe 5% more. So, it's not down to one gene, but a tortuously complex series of genetic factors."

"So, there's no such thing as a 'gay gene', but there are multiple 'gay genes'?" asks Mark.

"Not exactly. My position is that most aspects of human behaviour are attributable in part to genetic factors. But, looking to genetics to explain sexuality, makes about as much sense as looking at, I don't know, someone's diet to explain their taste in music."

"Well you know what they say," says George, "'you are what your mother ate!'"

"In which case both Richard and I are Tom Yum soup!" jokes Mark.

"Thank you, brother," says Richard, impatiently. "If we can't look at genetics, or diet," he says, turning mockingly towards his twin, "then where can we look? I still want to know why twins can differ so much in such a fundamental area as sexuality."

"Well," says Hugo, "sexuality is a spectrum, right, that's affected both by our biology and our experiences. So, there must have been an accumulation of factors, maybe infinitesimally small factors, that meant you went in one direction, Richard, and Mark went in another. That's what I'd say."

"Speaking of directions," says George, "Does anyone have any idea where we are?"

"I was following Clara," answers Hugo.

"Me too," the twins add in unison.

As they all turn to look at me, I say, "Don't worry, boys, I have everything completely under control." And for a moment, I even believe myself.

Chapter Fourteen

"Do you remember," asks George, "when we had to clean the older boys' shoes? Or do their shopping? Or warm the toilet seat for them!?"

We have settled in the living room, drinks in hand, after a dinner dominated by talk of politics. Now, as seems to happen so often with them, the boys are back to reminiscing about their schooldays.

"Of course," says Hugo, "there was a whole bloody points system for ranking the 'slaves'."

"You know, once I actually rounded all the younger boys up and told them, 'you don't have to do this, if you work together you can stop it!'" I look at Arthur as he reminisces, amused to think of him as a teenage rebel. "Unbelievably," he continues, "they all said 'no'. They actually *liked* being treated that way."

"Well, public school has always been a bit kinky," offers Richard, puncturing debate as always with sly humour.

"Well, in a way, it's human nature," says Hugo, ignoring Richard's attempt to derail the conversation. "We're like animals, looking towards leaders and finding security in our position in a power structure, even if it is a subservient position. Some people, it seems, don't want to be liberated."

"Or maybe," replies Arthur, "they want to achieve their own freedom but not the freedom of others. Look at the US. The American Dream offers people the hope of rising through the ranks and, in doing so, it ensures they're invested in maintaining the status quo."

"Exactly," I chime in. "They'd rather become the rich oppressor themselves than dismantle the system of oppression."

"Yes!" I'm flattered by Arthur's enthusiastic agreement. "It's just like at school," he continues. "Basically, what the younger boys thought was, 'These are the rules, so if I play by them I'll succeed'. And that idea became so ingrained that, by the time they were old enough to have 'slaves' of their own, they happily went along with it because they thought that was just the way things were."

"Of course, once they leave school, most of them do end up being very successful, but really it's only one in a hundred who becomes truly powerful."

"Aren't you overthinking this, chaps?" asks Richard. "Wasn't it just all peer pressure? No-one wanted to break ranks and, so to speak, 'let the side down'. The same is true in the wider world. It's hard to challenge the system around you when you're afraid of what the reprisals might be."

"True," says Hugo. "But that thinking is what allows dictators to take control. You just have to be ambitious enough to challenge the system for your own ends but do so in a way that means no-one notices the system is actually changing."

"Before it's too late," says Arthur.

"Like a frog in a pot of water," I observe. "If the water's cold when he goes in, he won't notice it slowly begin to boil…"

*

I am in constant awe
of the chase,

An unquenchable want
for the arbitrary

singular moments of a
rippling
ever partial
chasm of appeasements.
And then the
unconscious redistribution
of desires.

What grotesque
p o w e r
over our consciousness
stealing
precious stretches of
our brief existence.

We succumb and
deliver
our life
to an abstract
sequence of pleasures.

*

I am stunned by the expectations of our society. We have never had such easy access to such an abundance of knowledge. And yet I feel as though the majority of us are living, tagging along, ignorantly playing a part in one big Spiel. In my eyes, the most important missing element is the act of questioning. To question anything and everything, down to the root of its existence.

The accidental art of opinion is the thing that grips my mind again and again. Even as I write this, I wonder what others would think of the words on these pages. What meaning they would have. That is interesting, the fact that although a part of us will always be a socialized condemner, I do believe that somewhere very deeply opinions can exist beyond that. Most individuals, almost all, reading a poem will have understood its surface meaning. It is a simple allusion to certain things that we all know and experience. It references a life that we are all living, elements of our culture and society, even just the words or maybe some unoriginal phrasing.

There are so many different realities that compromise this one universe; so many beliefs that presuppose or contradict each other; disciplines and values that layered together form societies and communities. No matter how fervently one believes in our own reality, someone else is doing the same. Their conviction and your conviction are all we need to prove to social construction; that it is all a mystery. Religious belief systems are progressively attacked with more aggressively convincing scientific proof. And although there is proof, these concoctions are so loopy that there is space for the truth to be true and for the belief system to exist alongside it.

I am not religious. To me, science is a soothing balm. The fact that things can be quantified, reconstructed, proven and based on existing facts, leads me to believe that some things are in our control. That if things are understood, they are malleable. But no matter how much evidence we find, our universe will always remain a mystery. Last week, I read about the possibility of our lives being part of a simulation. When taking a logical, deductive approach from general rules, this is a realistic possibility. So, what do we do with this uncertainty? Most children grow up in a world that is not questioned. This is not only the case in religious families, in which the particular religion is transferred onto the next generation, but it is also the case in almost any other family. It is in mine. We are born into a life and that becomes our world. There will be ideals or particular people that you strive after. There will be rules that you adhere to. There will be norms that are 'normal' to you and quirks that are 'quirks' to you. Without the capacity to look beyond what your community calls normal and what other communities call normal, you can become locked into a system of thought. Your life will evolve; some things may be questioned, but you will always have some of that system in you and most will carry it on to their descendants.

There is not much you can do but construct your own reality. This might be achieved through reading and studying all the different realities that have been constructed and either putting together your different parts to make your own or discarding it all. When alone, we are probably more honest, but even then, it is almost impossible to be completely truthful as we absentmindedly make allowances and justifications. Wilde writes that the aim of life is self-development and understanding one's natural self, beyond borrowed sins and influences. That people are in fact, scared of themselves. Although written in a different age, it is so applicable. We don't look deep into the truth of what our soul is telling us, instead we fight for superficial strivings.

Inscribed in my copy of *The Picture of Dorian Gray*, a friend has written: "*To Clara, a book in which we all should feel revealed...*"

And she is right.

Chapter Fifteen

I turn to him now and observe the soft features of his face in the morning sunlight. He has such large green eyes covered by thick eyelashes.

"Hey you." His eyes slowly open.

"Hey yourself." I smile.

I begin to feel the tugging urge to share some of the swirl of thoughts that circle my mind every day. My life is intimately mine. Of course, I have shared snippets with others, but I have always kept the most important stories of my soul to myself. I wonder what it would be like to share them completely and with someone who felt only loyal to you, someone who would know your depths, who would dive deeper and deeper and deeper into the blues of your innermost centre. Though the thought is frightening, it is enticingly testing: would I want to tie myself to a person that way? The golden centre of my innermost self is shining and hot and my most treasured possession. Once shared it might still be there, but if not shared with the right person, it is tarnished. It loses its value every time it is uttered into the world. It is like when you sometimes overcome a seemingly insurmountable threshold and share something secret and the reaction is anticlimactic: you feel devalued, ridiculed. And yet right at this moment I feel ready to share.

I think of a few lines I once read by the German writer Thomas Glavinic:

Niemals vergessen, niemals vergessen, aber manches ist zu groß und zu wertvoll um

es behalten zu können, und man kann es nie-
mals berichten, auch sich selbst nicht. Es war
in der Sekunde weg, in der es gekommen war,
es gehörte ihnen nur in genau der Sekunde,
in der es passierte.

Which translates as:

Never forget, never forget, but some
things are too big and too valuable to remem-
ber, and you can never re-tell them, not even
to yourself. It was gone in the second it oc-
curred, it was theirs for just that one second
in which it happened.

This morning, waking up next to Arthur, is one such
moment. And yet I keep my thoughts in, my heart guard-
ing them fiercely, not giving in to the tug of my weak,
wishful mind.

*

It is very early, and still dark, as we get ready to go
hunting. The boys are already sitting at the kitchen table,
eyes half closed and sipping black coffee. They are wearing tweed blazers and shirts under vests. I am wearing
olive-coloured trousers with boots and a white blouse under a green and beige chequered coat. We wear hats with
bright orange rims, to signal our location to each other.
Although I grew up hunting, and it was always part of
my family's way of life, it is difficult for me, morally. In
Germany, pheasant hunting is almost non-existent,
thanks to the destruction of their natural habitats in order

to increase field sizes in the 1970s. However, every land-owner with more than one hundred hectares to their name is required by law to hunt wild animals such as deer. They can either do this themselves or they can pay hunters. The reason for this is that many wild animals no longer have natural predators, so if their numbers were to increase, the ecological equilibrium would be upended even further.

A traditional, ethical hunter is usually a farmer who knows the animals and the land inside out. He wakes up every morning during the hunting season and waits for the buck he wants to shoot. He knows exactly which one it is and has observed it over many years, fed it when it was younger and kept it healthy. It is exactly the right time, the buck is possibly already ill or weak, and he kills it as the sun comes up. The buck dies immediately, because he is a good hunter and shoots in the right place. Many argue that hunting only becomes immoral when it becomes a social affair and is not thought out, careful and controlled. In Britain, the pheasants are often bought and bred purely to be hunted. They are fed and trained to fly high – as they would usually fly low – so that hobby hunters can shoot upwards to kill. The pheasants are rarely eaten, and mostly thrown away.

These thoughts are on my mind as we divide into pairs. Richard and I go off in one of the Land Rovers. We drive in the cold morning air, a layer of white mist hanging over the fields. We settle at a small opening with a high seat. Fernanda has prepared little baskets with blankets and flasks of tea and oat biscuits. We sit in silence, taking in the beauty of the morning. At first, the silence is natural, friendly. But the longer it lasts, the more apparent it becomes, to me at least, that Richard and I don't know each other well enough for us to sit in silence without it feeling awkward. A loud silence.

"How do you feel about hunting?" I ask, more to give voice to my own thoughts than to solicit his.

"I'm not a huge fan, to be totally honest," answers Richard.

"Really? That surprises me."

"Why?" he asks, smiling, "because you thought I was such a massive Tory?" He laughs good-naturedly at my obvious discomfort. "You should know by now, Clara, that I am exactly the type of Englishman who holds almost everything and everyone in utter contempt, including my own class."

"So, you dislike hunting because of its political connotations?"

"Essentially. I hate all the crap that goes along with it. But what I do enjoy about it is the skill it takes. That's exactly what attracted me to the idea of joining the army: the skill of the soldier."

"I can't imagine ever wanting to join the army, or understand the mindset of someone who does enlist."

"It's a vocation, like any other, and it totally absorbs you. I don't like the idea of being on the periphery. Of being unnecessary. I like the idea that as a junior officer you have a responsibility to your men. They have all sorts of troubles and you help them with their daily lives. It's much more of a management role, even a pastoral role, than a military one. It's a serious wakeup call to the way the other half live and what they go through."

"It must be very humbling, when people come to you with their problems."

"Absolutely. I feel a responsibility to my platoon, not to my country. It's like Yeats said: 'Those that I fight I do not hate, / Those that I guard I do not love'. And yes, before you ask, I am aware of the irony of quoting an Irish nationalist to explain my feelings towards the British military."

I feel unmoored listening to Richard speaking. In company, he can be such a boor, brash and almost bullying in his sneering sense of humour. But one on one, he's much more complex than I had imagined. There is still so much about him I can never agree with, but for a moment, I find myself warming to him.

"How can you square the pride you take as an individual with the actions you're taking, the lives you're destroying, at the behest of a state you say you disdain?"

"Easily. When you fight...no, when you live only for yourself and those closest to you, it is utterly immaterial what impact you have on others. That's the same reason why I couldn't care less if some protester takes it upon themselves to sabotage a hunt. It's their business. I may disdain the apparatus of the state, but not the state itself, because I'm connected to my country on an emotional level."

"Couldn't you still feel that emotional connection without 'the apparatus of the state', as you say, and the borders that ultimately prompt conflict between one nation and another?"

"Of course," he says, "but it makes sense for nations to be organised as single units. I remember when I was studying PPE there was this one module where we focused on what it means to be 'good sized nation'. On the one hand, you want to provide public goods: security, schools, legal systems and so forth. It really makes sense to have a large group of people because you don't have to rethink each system every time. On the other hand, if the entity is too large you may have too many regionally diverging preferences, cultures, or languages."

"Like the UK, you mean? I ask.

"Quite. At the end of the day, it's difficult to rationalise something as inherently irrational as national sentiment. It's like families. Children naturally want to love their parents, even when it's abundantly clear their parents might not be worthy of love. By the same token, people want to feel proud of their country because it's their place of origin, or their home."

"But there are also so many things that we have to be ashamed of, and that's where the issues begin. Nationalism turns negative if it's being used or abused by politicians in order to cement their power at the expense of others."

"You're quite right, Clara. Nationalism is only powerful if it goes hand in hand with respect for those who have other beliefs and other forms of government. Nevertheless, I would fight for my country if I had to. It's human instinct: I care more about my family than my neighbours. Humans always need to differentiate between those who are close to them and those who are not."

I think about this: the economic need for nation states. But I think it goes beyond that. It is also important in life and human conduct to have certain concepts to work with, no matter whether they are true or not. Or it becomes too abstract. Pooling individuals into different groups, so that we can think about them and order them to help humans think in 'us and them' terms. Different countries and national entities help make sense of life and to make sense of reality. To know who to trust and not to trust. I'm not sure whether we still need nation states and borders: it is simply that we are used to thinking in those terms. Nationalism simplifies a world that is getting more and more complicated.

Richard shoots a buck and I shudder a little.

"Well done!" I exclaim.

"Thank you, Clara! I'm pretty sure I haven't heard any shots from the others yet." He grins, revelling in his own success.

Chapter Sixteen

Richard is the only one who shot anything. After a late brunch prepared by Fernanda, we fall back into bed for a nap. Slowly one after another we wake up and trod downstairs to join the others sunbathing on the terrace. Arthur has been in his atelier all day since the hunt. As I walk up towards the studio, I spot him standing in front of his studio looking out into the sea of lavender and green. Without announcing myself, Arthur turns around, having sensed my presence behind him. I have never understood how we can notice the slightest reshuffling of air around us without looking. But we always do.

"Hey you."

"Hey yourself."

"Where have you been? I've hardly seen you all day."

"I got lost in my thoughts and, before I knew it, I wandered further than I'd intended."

"Look at me." His voice is soft. "Stop wandering, Clara."

"What do you mean?"

"You can stop searching."

"Searching for what?"

"Answers. You have so many questions gnawing away at you. One minute, you're here; the next minute, your mind tears you away and you get lost in a labyrinth."

He's not pitying me. He's not patronizing me. He understands that I can't float through life with ease. But he doesn't understand that this is who I am and not something that can be altered.

"I can't stop, Arthur. How do you manage not to wander in the way I do?"

"I've learned to accept that there are things we'll simply never know or understand."

"I don't think I can do that."

"Of course you can. Let me show you."

He turns towards me and takes my hands in both of his. With one hand, he holds mine, supporting them from below. With the other, he traces my fingers, one at a time. Then he locks our hands together.

"Look at me." I look up into his green eyes. Golden specks surround his pupils and catch the light. Green and gold and a little bit of black. They are all I see in that moment.

"I am here," he says. "I am here, in this moment, with you."

"Yes."

"Are you happy?"

"I am happy." I smile.

"So, those are two things we know. We are here and we are happy."

"Yes, we know those two things."

"There are many things we don't know. Many more things. How we got here. How we have evolved. Why we do certain things."

I interrupt him. "Yes, why…"

"– Yes, why," he continues. "But we have to know when to stop asking and when to find a way to be present without needing a reason."

He pulls me closer towards him, untangles our hands and cups my head. It seems small in his hands.

"You will always be asking. You will always be searching. But even if you understood the intricacies of this whole world, how would that change this moment? I am holding you and we are happy. Whatever the reason for this feeling, it is true. And is there anything bigger than that? Is there anything bigger than feeling this way?"

*

Our bodies lie intertwined on the cold atelier floor. My head is in the nook of his arms and my nose is pressed against his chest. I can smell that beautiful, earthy scent of clean skin after a long day. It reminds me of summers swimming in the Mediterranean and licking the salt from my fingers.

A calm has settled over my soul and I stand up, leaving my scattered clothes on the floor. Rays of golden light are filtering through the glass gaps in the walls as I walk amongst the figures, letting my hands trace their curves. The sun is dancing, bouncing from limb to limb, as though the statues are talking to each other. Communicating their affection to one another. Intrigued, I stop at a wooden sculpture. Unlike the other womanlike shapes, it resembles a knot. Upon closer inspection, the soft walnut could be a woman curled up into a ball. Her back is arched over contracted thighs and arms. An uncontrollable desire to uncurl the figure comes over me. I want to find its soul and tell it to relax. I want to pull out her legs and then stretch out the arms so that she can dance with the others. So that the light can find its way to the grooves of her wood and smoothen them.

Arthur walks up behind me and kisses my shoulder. "Like it?"

"I do. It's beautiful." I walk through the women, until I find my twin. "And I like this one."

"Do you?" His gaze, usually so certain, has softened.

I study the dark, reddish clay that shapes my body and stand behind it, laughing. "Do you want to make any adjustments?"

Arthur mockingly picks up a scraping tool and waves it around. I reach up and stop his hand in midair. "Don't do that," I say quietly. "I love her." I surprise myself with my own reaction.

"That's a beautiful thing to hear."

"What's going to happen to her?"

"I don't know yet." His face becomes serious. "I have an exhibition coming up in a few months...although I'm not sure if that would be the right occasion for her."

"Why not?" I laugh.

He sighs a little and runs his hands through his hair. "It's complicated." He looks away, as though he is searching for the right words in the air. "I have been commissioned by an Arab client to create a whole range of statues, first to be exhibited for a few months and then to be displayed in his home. I'm not sure how you would feel about being displayed in his home."

"That's interesting. What's his name?"

"Ahmad Hassan. He's a well-known oil mogul."

"Never heard of him."

"He was actually in the countryside with some of his wives this weekend and is going to drop by at some point this afternoon to have a final look at the pieces and make any last requests."

"Can clients request amendments?" I ask, looking around at the women in this room that have somehow become meaningful to me.

"Well...they can express wishes and depending on how accommodating the artist is," saying this, Arthur winks at me, "we usually find a way to work something out."

I hear my name being called from somewhere in the distance. "We're all going on a walk now." I pull Arthur towards me and kiss him. "Good luck with this Ahmad guy. I'm sure he'll love it all."

*

City Country

The echoing stench
of opinion
borrowed thoughts
inescapable influences, and
superficial strivings.

A rigor routine
governed by
the guiding fences
of an
all-knowing
unforgiving
city.

Yielded temptations.

Away from these distractions
sorrow
of a deeper kind
l a t c h
themselves
onto your, now,
bare
soul.

Islands

of time
give way to
an inquisition
taking apart
what was once
seemingly stain-
less.

All this might only
wash away
if you give yourself completely
to the overlapping pale green
crescents of
nature's
monastery.

Chapter Seventeen

It is my favourite time of the day. The sky is peach coloured and white slashes seep into the yellowing tie dye of the sky. The hot air of the day is slowly cooling down and a soft breeze slips under my blouse, relieving me of a weight that I didn't even know was there before. I walk towards the house and my eyes drift towards the glass windows of Arthur's studio. It is not until I walk a little closer that I recognise Arthur in a very crisp looking navy suit. A plump, rather short man wearing a long white cotton robe is walking between the sculptures. His fingers lingering on some. A red and white gingham tablecloth-like sheet crowns his bearded head. The two men are conversing as though they are friends. Hassan seems to be pleased with the sculptures, smiling as he takes photos of some. Arthur is backed against the wall, looking almost child-like with a teacher in the room. I wonder why it is that some people have such a presence of power that anyone, no matter how confident, wordlessly respects them. I was never such a person. Some people recognised that I thought and questioned things, but that raw, wordless respect was never on the cards. Maybe when you smile too much, people don't take you as seriously.

Looking at Arthur, so visibly full of apprehension, immediately takes some of my respect for him away. I used to think that artists created their work out of pure inspiration and that was it. I thought that they were immune to power plays; immune to influence and opinion. But here I am presently, staring at Hassan who has by now arrived at my sculpture and stops. His hands move up my legs and clasp my waist. Pushing upwards they cup my breasts. I gasp a little, feeling vulnerable and physically touched. I have to put my own hands over my breasts to remind myself that this is me, what he has, is a copy of myself. The fingers of one of his hands are now sprawled over my face. The palm covering my eyes. I look towards Arthur, who playfully pushes himself off the wall and towards Hassan. Hassan is telling him something which I cannot make out and throws one of his arms over Arthur's shoulders. They are now both standing in front of my sculpture, bodies linked, examining. Hassan eventually brings his hands back to about fifty centimetres from my breasts and gestures some sort of bigger motion. Laughingly, Arthur takes a pen and circles my breast on the sculpture, taking some sort of note, as though he were some sort of plastic surgeon. I feel a rush of anger overcome me and I turn away to walk towards the main house. The desire to leave for London, a sad thought before, is suddenly urgent and pressing. I cannot get the mogul's hands out of my mind. His hands on my breasts. His hands on my face. And his hands on Arthur's back.

I pull off my boots in the entryway and bound towards the stairs, when I hear whispers coming from the kitchen.

"Fernanda?" I call out. The voices quiet down at the sound of my call, but no reply. I walk into the kitchen and see three women sitting at the kitchen table. Each of them is wearing a long black cloak, which covers all but their hands and face. Their hair is hidden under a separate piece of more of the same black cloth.

"Hello", I say to their silently staring faces.

"Good evening." One of the ladies stands up a little and, though formally, confidently reaches out her hand to greet me.

"Hello. My name is Clara. I'm assuming you are here with Hassan?" I ask.

"Yes. We're his wives," the same lady says, but does not offer her own name. "He is with your husband, I think."

"Arthur's not my husband!" I laugh and, suddenly self-conscious about my slightly openly cut blouse, button up another button. "I'm just here to visit." Ignoring the slightly confused faces, I offer them a cup of tea. After I pour a cup of mint tea for each of the women, I sit next to the lady who spoke to me. The other two silently speak to each other in a language that I cannot understand, and then look back at me.

"So, I hear that you have spent the weekend in the countryside. Did you enjoy yourself?"

"Yes. We did, it was beautiful. I love being outside."

"I do too. It is stunning here." It is quiet and the conversation is struggling to flow. I suddenly regret sitting down and the feeling of anger, for what I just saw, rises up in my throat again. Looking, searching into the greenish tea, I remind myself of my mother who always makes any conversation interesting by just asking. Asking whatever comes to her mind that would be the most interesting thing that person could share. I look into their beautiful faces, framed by blackness and ask: "How do you find living in London?"

As though sensing the courage that it took for me to ask this seemingly simple question, the woman replies honestly: "It is a beautiful city, but it can be difficult for us."

"Difficult how?"

"I feel like I'm sort of a stranger," she says firmly. "Like I don't belong here, even though I was born and raised here."

"What part of yourself do you feel doesn't belong?" I look her in the eye, trying to communicate some sort of solidarity.

"You know, I feel like I'm always having to prove myself just for what my religion stands for, do you know what I mean?"

"I can only imagine..." I start, before she interrupts. I feel like I have opened a faucet and her words rush out like trapped water.

"I just feel like, I don't know, I just feel like an outsider and it's not a nice feeling, because people already think they know you without knowing you. Just because of my religion." She pauses, thinking. "But it's not so much what my religion stands for, rather what people perceive it to be. They don't want to open their minds. They don't really want to learn about Islam. They just want to look and judge from the outside. I wasn't aware of this when I was younger, but as I've grown up, I've had my eyes opened. So, I know now that what I wear either makes me a victim or a threat. The public sees us as Muslims, not as individuals...and then you just have to live with the people who aren't going to give you a chance, people who've already made up their minds. That's when a smile from a stranger on the street can mean more than anything in the world."

There is a pause, while I struggle to think how to respond. Finally, I manage to muster a hesitant: "Can I ask you something?"

"Of course."

"Do you think..." I dare to ask, not quite sure how the question will be received. "...Do you think that if you were a Christian, people would be more welcoming?"

"Okay, let's say I lose Islam. Now, I've lost one target...but wait, I still have another target that is just as big.

I am not the same shade as you are. If I bleach, maybe, just maybe, my problems might be coloured over too."

"Can you bleach yourself?" I ask, rather incredulously.

"Yes, of course you can. It's very easy to bleach yourself, and exceptionally cheap. But that would be like losing my...myself. But, all the same, many consider it as an option, all so that they can try to become a part of," she gestures to our surroundings, "all this."

"All this..." I repeat, thinking out loud.

She looks at me, intently, and says: "Look at you. You fit into 'all this'. You slot right into the classic Western standard of beauty: white skin, blue eyes, blonde hair, small waist..."

"I understand your point, but is 'all this'," – as I repeat her phrase I rather self-consciously gesture towards my own figure – "a racialised ideal or a gendered ideal? Isn't female beauty always circumstantial and individual? Women will always have something they wish to change, to attune, to edit...I mean, don't you think that it's easier for guys because they're not held to the same standards? I feel like my brother is always regarded as the same person, no matter how his appearance changes. You know, it's like if they're a bit fat or a bit thin, no-one cares. Whereas girls are always judged and are always judging themselves. What is that saying? Men age like wine and women age like grapes."

"Yes, it's always been women, women, women..." She repeats the word, and it plays in my mind like a loop: *women, women, women...*

"I have to be honest, when Arthur told me he was working with Ahmad Hassan, the first thing I thought of was how badly women are oppressed in the Middle East.

But maybe I'm just as bad, judging another culture from the outside, setting my values as the benchmark?"

"I think you've hit the nail on the head. The reason so many people in the West think we're oppressed is because we don't, or won't, conform to your ideals. We're not a slave to society, we're not going to wear what you want, we're not trying to prove ourselves as beautiful. We know that we're beautiful and we believe that it's shallow to think that beauty depends on the way you dress or on how you are seen by others. I don't have to wear something short and revealing to feel beautiful. When I cover my head, I don't feel oppressed, I feel liberated."

"In what way?" I ask, almost incredulous.

"Look at it this way. I don't wear it because Allah tells me to, but I wear it as a sign of my personal devotion to Allah. When I wear it, I feel His protection, like a shield. Now, there was a time when religion was the protagonist in the story of the world, but now it's the antagonist. To some people, atheists, secular humanists, even Christians, religious belief is seen as acquiescence to a form of oppression. But I believe in my religion, I'm okay with who I am, and I don't need a saviour."

"Isn't that easy for you to say, though, when you're here rather than back home? For all the faults with how you, and women like you, are seen here, don't you enjoy greater freedoms here? Can you truly say you're at peace with your country?"

"Listen, every country has its failings, and my country's not different. There are many things that need to change. But the things that my mother and grandmother had to endure are shifting...As I said, I love my hijab. It's my choice to wear it, and if I were to remove it right now, that would be my choice too. I do in fact think that we are moving forward, in your terms, and maybe our increased presence in the West will, finally, make us feel a little more accepted. A little better able to navigate 'all this'."

"Hopefully. Do you work?" I ask.

"No, we don't." The lady firmly replies for all three. The youngest-looking of the three flinches a little and catches my eye. I have never seen such stark, open green eyes in my life before.

"Would you like to?" I ask without thinking that I am doing precisely what the woman had told me, made her feel like an outsider. The feeling of being represented as a victim of their own culture. As I try to search for something to say to save myself, Hassan walks into the room with Arthur following closely behind. His gown floats around him and he looks almost god-like. His presence takes up the whole room as he says something unintelligible to the women. His three wives start to collect their things and stand up.

"Good Evening. My name is Ahmad." He stretches out his hand towards me and looks earnest.

"Hello…er…, good evening," I stutter. My face goes bright red and a part of me understands Arthur's behaviour in the presence of such a powerful aura. Everyone is rustling, bustling and moving around. I look at Arthur who turns away from me, not being able to meet my eye.

"We are just leaving. Lovely art. Are you coming to the exhibition?" And at that moment, I feel Hassan study my face and possibly, even recognition flash over his own. He turns to look at Arthur and winks. His eyes are back on me, but now run down my body. I feel bare. His hand reaches to my shoulder and he leaves it resting there. Heavy.

"I would hope so." Arthur replies for me.

"Definitely. You must be there!" Ahmad laughs and lets his hand slide down, grazing my waist and ever so slightly touching my behind. A fingertip of contact, if not less. Probably unnoticeable to anyone else, but after seeing him with my sculpture it shakes me. He throws his hands in the air and starts to walk out of the door, with Arthur and his wives following suit. I stand at the kitchen table, holding onto the edge of the wood. I look down and realise my knuckles are white and clutching the wood tightly. So tightly as though I fear that if I let go, I will fall. I feel as though I will be sick.

"My name is Zafira." The woman with whom I had eye contact has stayed behind and looks at me with her bright eyes.

"What a beautiful name." I get the words out, although still in some state of shock.

"I like Clara. It sounds so clear. Cla-ra." She pronounces my name out loud.

"Thank you." I smile at Zafira.

"I would like to."

"What would you like?"

"Work. You asked if we would like to work. I would like to. I would like to work."

"Oh," I say, unable to get anything else of meaning out. Stunned by her candor, I ask: "What would you like to do? Maybe I can help. I am sure it is difficult to find something in times like these."

"I studied biology. I would do anything, anything to move ahead."

"I have just the person for you. I will put you into contact with a friend of mine called Hugo. He does research at UCL. He is also here but is still out on a walk. Why don't you give me your number and we can work something out?"

Her face lights up at my words and darkens just the same. "I suppose I could give you my number, but my husband has strict rules. I'm afraid, it most likely won't work. But I would like to see you again sometime." She takes a pen from the kitchen island and jots down her number on the side of a discarded copy of the *Financial Times*. As she writes, Hassan comes back into the kitchen and speaks roughly in the same language that I did not understand before. He takes her hand and leads her towards the door. She trips a little on her dress and he mutters something under his breath, turning around to look at me. I run out behind them and Zafira quickly takes my hand and squeezes it, before getting into the car. Her eyes are pleading, but her face is composed. Serene.

Chapter Eighteen

I stand on the gravel, pressing my feet into the ground, not sure what I just witnessed in these last moments. I go back inside and google 'Ahmad Hassan'. Multiple search results come up. Most describe the successes of his oil businesses. As I search further down into dated articles, I find an older article with a picture of Hassan with multiple women around him in a Mayfair club. The title reads *SUBMISSION GOING TOO FAR? WHEN CULTURAL DIFFERENCES BREAK OUR LAWS AT HOME.* I skim the article: a suspected, but strenuously denied, case of sexual assault. His response: no comment.

Arthur walks in my direction, apprehension etched in his face.

"So? What did you think?" As he asks me, he carries on walking towards the studio, gesturing for me to follow. I follow.

"Let me get this straight, and please correct me if I am wrong: Ahmad Hassan, an oil mogul powerful in a country, a country in which women are generally treated like...like...possessions, and who himself has been accused of sexual assault, has commissioned you to create sculptures of nude women to be displayed in his home?!" I am surprised by my own reaction. Stark and loud, towards this man that I am only just getting to know.

My eyes dart around the studio. Before me, the women suddenly look revealed. Exposed. Naked. My gaze lands on the figure resembling myself. *I love her*, I think. A moment ago, I had felt so accepted, so understood, so secure. Now I am disgusted by my own emotions. My actions. My naïveté.

"Listen, Clara. He's much more progressive than you realise. You can't believe everything you read. Don't overthink this." I silently look away, unable to meet his eyes. "I questioned this all too, initially. But I've decided to do this. It's not like I'm doing this for selfish gain. I'm giving a lot of the money to Hugo's lab. Think about all the good that money can do!"

"It doesn't change the fact that by taking his money you are basically endorsing this man's way of life. The way he treats his wives. The way he treats women!" I shudder at the memory of his eyes on me.

"What about the research that I'm endorsing? He already made that money, so why shouldn't I spend it on something that matters? It's better in my hands than keeping it in his! Anyway, if I don't take it, he'll just find another artist who will."

"That's beside the point. The point is that you, YOU, are accepting it and that reflects YOUR values as a person." I am overwhelmed with emotion, struggling to understand what it is that I am feeling. Why do I care so much what this man does, what values he endorses, when I have only known him for one week? "Arthur, if you were to reject his commission, publicly, it would be a hundred times more valuable than the money you are taking."

"I can't do that, Clara, it's too late." As he speaks, I watch him deftly opening the gold buttons of his blazer. "Look, what if we give him the benefit of the doubt and trust him when he says he wants to change his ways; change his country?"

"So, you knew? I just quickly searched the articles, but I also saw the way he was with his wives. The way he was with me."

"Yes of course. I did my research. But like I said, he denies a lot and wants to change his country generally."

"Seriously? All he's doing is throwing a party in a fancy gallery so all the politicians and financiers he invites will think how cultured he is and swallow his propaganda about how wonderfully progressive things are at home."

"How can you say that? This man is the face of modern and new Arabs, coming to learn and mix with us. He is the icon for the next generation of Arabs to look up to, and believe that their country can be more egalitarian than ever before. I want to support that progress. But I can't do that if I reject this opportunity."

"The country still supports the death penalty, stoning, and hundreds of brutally convicted women who spoke out against their mistreatment are still in their prisons. They have even linked him to ordering the death, no…let me correct myself…the bone-sawing, of a journalist who wrote negatively about him."

"Oh, come on. How many people have the USA killed and no one cares?"

"I don't think the USA, no matter how hard they might come down on civil liberties, would ever do to a journalist what your friends do."

"That's incredibly naïve, Clara."

"Well, I may be naïve but at least I know my own hands are clean."

"Clean? Do you think that any of us, with our privileged lifestyles, can really say our hands are clean? Anyway, who are we to judge? Their religion, their culture and their laws are different to ours. We're talking about a feudal system where the king is not just a head of state but a leader to be served. We might both think that a lot of what goes on over there is wrong, but we are viewing things by our standards, not theirs. They could just as easily look at everything that's wrong with Britain and judge us."

"Oh for God's sake, Arthur. The USA and Russia both have different laws, cultures, and even religions, compared to us, but we'll readily criticise them. Are you saying we shouldn't criticise Hassan's country when they do something abhorrent?"

"Yes! Frankly, we haven't got a leg to stand on when it comes to judging other countries. Clara, this is colonialism of the mind! Who are we as a Western democracy to impose our views and democracy on others because we think it's right? In colonialist times, we went out to civilise people, thinking that we were better, when in fact *we* were the barbarians, treating people like animals. Maybe we're better than that now, maybe, but just think about the inequalities in this country today. Look at all the problems we've discussed this past week! Class, healthcare, education. What about the sexism that's still endemic here? And you presume to criticise them? Tell me, do their 'oppressed' women actually want to uncover? Have you spoken to any of them? The assumptions you're making are not better than colonialism of the mind."

"Excuse me, colonialism of the mind? I'm not saying we should go over there and change their way of life. What I'm saying is that I don't endorse their objectification and mistreatment of women. The women may very well say that wearing the hijab is a choice. But when not wearing one, would mean God only knows what type of punishment, you can't tell me that's a real choice."

"We're going round in circles, Clara. Whatever the rights and wrongs of their country, or ours, the fact is I'm not taking Hassan's money for my own selfish gain. You're forgetting that I want to do something good with it. You're the one who's always searching for meaning; searching for some kind of grand explanation for everything. Don't you think the money I'll give to Hugo's research could do some good?"

"Of course it could do some good, but it doesn't change the fact that his money is, and always will be, bad. Using bad money to do good things doesn't wipe the moral slate clean. It compromises everything. Remember when that journalist uncovered all those men from the Presidents Club groping waitresses at fundraising events? Those men thought that they could do whatever they wanted because they were donating so much money to Great Ormond Street Hospital. But when the story broke, the hospital said that they didn't want anything to do with the money."

"That's different."

"What's so different about it?! Hassan is doing far more than groping women, I can tell you that!

"It's different because I'm not doing any of those things myself! All I'm doing is effectively greenwashing."

"Oh and greenwashing is totally fine now, is it?"

"It isn't really greenwashing. I didn't mean that."

"Then, what are you doing? I'll tell you what you're doing, you're doing something that will cast a shadow over your entire career. Think about the message you're sending. You're not just selling your work to the highest bidder, you're selling yourself. If you rejected this offer, you could say to the world that you're not just someone who produces beautiful works of art, but someone who wants his work to mean beautiful things."

"That sounds very noble. But beautiful things don't help anyone. This money can. How many people would

I be helping if I take the money, compromise my principles, and sacrifice my career to help the research being done by far better people than me?"

"You think very highly of yourself for someone who excuses the oppression of all Arab women!"

"Clara! Come on. Not all women..."

"Even if it were only one woman, you will still have it on your conscience that."

"Listen, all I know is that by taking the money I can make sure it does some good. If I go back on my word, my conscience might be a little cleaner, but nothing would have changed. Do you really think he will change his behaviour because I say, 'Thanks, but no thanks'?"

"Of course, he won't change everything because of you. But by taking this money you're making it harder for the next person to say no. And the person after that. You're a good person, Arthur. I might not have known you very long, but I think I know enough to see that. But what you're doing is making the world just that little bit easier for bad people to do what they like."

"I'm flattered, Clara, really. But I think you're overestimating my significance in the great scheme of things. I'm hardly headline news."

"You've been offered a solo exhibition at a respected gallery. Using that platform to take a stand would be headline news!"

"No, it wouldn't. Because when all's said and done, if I don't take it, someone else will. And they might not have the same motivation to use that money to help others. The media doesn't care about me. I'm not Banksy. I'm just some random guy making sculptures."

At that moment, Richard knocks on the door, announcing his presence out of courtesy to the row he must have heard raging within. Invigorated by our argument, I forgot what things must look like from the outside: two people, yelling at each other amongst nude statues.

"I'm so sorry to interrupt, but Hugo and I have to drive back to London and we wanted to say goodbye."

"Don't worry," I say. "I should be going too. I'll go pack my things," I say.

I am halfway out of the atelier when Arthur calls, "Wait."

"I'll give you two a moment," says Richard, diplomatically.

And then it is just the two of us again. I look at Arthur, standing there in the midst of his artworks, and remind myself that he is entitled to a different perspective. The fact that he has a view and an opinion, that is well thought out, is more than most people have.

"You're not a random guy, Arthur," I insist. "You are incredibly talented and you've obviously thought long and hard about your decision."

He smiles. "I have." With that bashful smile, I think he probably gets away with everything.

"I don't know why I am encouraging this now, but if you are going to invest the money, you should take advantage of the situation."

"And how should I do that?"

"Well, when we were younger, I remember that my parents sometimes rented out our house. My mother could not bear being in the Hamptons for two months and our house being empty, when it could be rented out and the money used for one of her projects. So, she would ask the renters to transfer the money directly into the charity, as that way it would be tax-free and double the amount for whatever the cause was."

"Very interesting. I will think about that."

"Yes, you should. Most of the time it even inspired the renters to put in some extra. I'm sure Hassan has some money to spare…"

"I'm sure he does."

"I'm going to go with the others now. Thank you for this beautiful weekend," I say softly.

He walks towards me. "Am I allowed to kiss you goodbye?"

I hesitate. "Yes."

And so he does. I wonder if I really have moral boundaries, or if all I have is a rough, easily malleable idea of right and wrong. I leave the room, without looking back at Arthur. He doesn't protest, or ask when we will see each other again, and I wonder if maybe I was too rash.

Chapter Nineteen

I am on the streets of London. Wandering. Wondering. I can't help thinking about the argument. You read about these things or hear about these conflicts, these dilemmas, you think about them theoretically. But it never occurs to you that you might be faced with a decision of right and wrong. A moral compass in your hand. What sequence of events had to occur, that Arthur can affect the way a very controversial nation is depicted in the media? I somehow feel trapped by the weight of another man's decision. There are so many moral dilemmas of this sort, that have been proposed by philosophers and philanthropists. If you could press a button that kills someone, but provides one million pounds for children in need, would you do it? I wouldn't, just like I wouldn't push the fat man to stop the trolley which would kill four strapped to the tracks.

No, I thought I could never get involved. And although this may not be quite as extreme as the death of a person, here I am getting involved. Here I am, challenging a culture that I do not even understand. And potentially halting some incredible genetic research. My dad always says: 'Stick to the rules'. Even if you buy stolen jewelry with honest money, return the jewelry, you want no part of that. Would Arthur really be supporting honest research with dirty money? Kundera wrote: 'There is no means of testing which decision is better, because there is no basis for comparison. We live everything as it comes…like an actor going on cold. And what can life be worth, if the first rehearsal for life is life itself?'

It is said that the greatest events of life occur in our minds. It is the battles in our head with fabricated fears that cause us the most pain. Words that are a construction of humanity can destroy us. It is because the mind touches and controls our senses, just like words do. And it is thus our senses that we need to grasp and try not to control, but instead simply admire and respect. We need to be smart about it; realising when they are being driven by forces that are irrelevant and when they are being touched by the power of people and matters we care about. In any case, whatever the emotion or sensory experience is, it is an experience in itself. Irrespective of the cause, it becomes a part of our being, a process that will shape some part of our soul. They manifest themselves in the creases of our forehead and the folds of our heart. We are quite the opposite of rational. If we were rational, we would not let social constructions and arbitrary ideals rule our minds and direct our lives. But although I understand this, I cannot apply it to my life. It is like advice that you desperately need to apply yourself but can only share with others. They are like New Year's resolutions. At the end of the day there is little that you can do to control your mind and the vigour of your emotional self. So possibly the deterministic view of life is right? Maybe there is little we can do to alter the path ahead.

*

The next day, I get a text from Arthur:

I'm back in the city. Dinner at mine tonight?

My heart jolts as I read the message. I reply about thirty minutes later, making sure to leave just enough time to not seem too eager. A hopeless game, which you can only lose.

Sounds good. Can I bring anything?

He replies within seconds:

Just yourself.

I take extra care getting ready, putting on a little too much makeup and taking the time to blow dry my hair so it falls in soft blonde waves. I wear a white, silk blouse, pairing it with a flared skirt and ruffled cream wedges.

I grab my tote and take the tube to Notting Hill. Apprehensive and a little sticky, I arrive at his familiar door. I ring the bell and moments later he is standing there. Quite unlike the week before, he is cleanly shaven and freshly showered, with not a trace of clay or paint on him.

"Hello you."

"Hello yourself," I respond, and there is a moment in which neither of us really know what to do, quite like our first date.

"Come in, come in," he urges, kissing me on each cheek.

I follow him through the beautiful arched doors to his whimsical garden. The bent and weathered wooden table outside is set with olive green plates and wine glasses.

"Can I interest you in some Merlot?"

"I would love some, thank you. How are you?"

"I'm great," he speaks as he opens the bottle. "I actually have some fantastic news. I spoke to Ahmad on the phone about your idea to put the money straight into Hugo's research fund and he was ecstatic."

"Really?!"

"Yes! And he had an even better idea."

"What do you mean?"

"Well, apparently he is already heavily invested in a different genetic research fund and said he would match the amount, effectively quadrupling the value if you consider the tax exemption!"

"Wow...I don't know what to say. Did you check it out?"

"What? The fund?"

"Yes."

"I did a quick Google search and it looks quite cool. It's a little more specialised in genetic engineering than Hugo's lab, but I kind of like that."

"Have you told Hugo?"

"No, I haven't yet, but I'm hoping he will understand that this makes quite a lot of sense."

We sit down at the table and Arthur gets out a cigarette. I hadn't seen him smoke before. He inhales deeply and turns away from me to blow out the smoke.

"I hope you don't mind." He gestures towards the cigarette in his one hand and puts the other on my knee.

"No, don't worry about it." I wave it off with a weak smile, slightly turning away from the direction of his smoke.

From that point on we engage in light, easy conversation. The sky lets the sun set into a darker evening hanging above us. Arthur kisses me, but it's different. I feel my lips on his. I search for it, for the feeling that I had the first time I kissed him. The excitement. His hands slide down my body and he picks me up, to carry me inside.

Sometimes I feel like I'm betraying love itself. But not this time. Sometimes you don't want to speak about certain things. You don't want to put it into words, out of fear that it might not come true.

Love is the most magical form of human connection, one that goes beyond what we can put into words. A look maybe can capture it. A touch can ignite it. If true, a connection between two souls exceeds the constructions of our world and enters a realm that can only be defined in bursting temperatures of colour and shivers.

The fear that I will not feel such an emotion consumes me at times. I wonder why we have such rigid expectations when all we want is that raw emotion. At the end of the day, that will always trump money and looks. That feeling that fills every crevice of your mind and soul, that reminds you every second of every day that you have a soul out there aligned with yours. Your mind and heart connected to the unspeakable magnitude of another. Whatever the other factors. Whatever it is. It is impossible to trump love. Yet so often, we fail to drop our guard at the threshold of something bigger.

I observe people all the time. I look at their faces and I look at the way they carry themselves, what they do to their body, their attire, their demeanour, the way their eyes study things, calculating odds, weighing options, adjusting to surroundings, falling into place between all the other pairs of eyes. What would happen if everything, anything we ever did, was determined by our search for, our capacity and willingness to fall truly in love? Is it inevitable that we will always get lost on the way in search of other successes, that some argue are just as, if not more, fulfilling, important, powerful than love?

I look at Arthur and I know it isn't love. I know that is what I want it to be. And somewhere, back deep inside of myself, I know that it will happen. Even if it will be too late, even if I will miss the opportunity or it remains unrequited. I know that I will feel love. As I stand here in his beautiful garden, I finally give in to the nudging of my soul. I let go of the force and touch his cheek.

"I have to go. I'm so sorry."

Arthur looks at me and knows too. Something like this does not slip between the cracks. We both know.

"Okay you...I..."

"Okay," I whisper.

"Bye." He pronounces the simple word slowly.

"Bye." I look at him and set us free from our days of intertwinement.

I close the door and stand outside in the cool night air. I look up and the stars are covered by a haze of cloud. But I know they are there. It begins to drizzle slightly and I let it creep into my hair and down my neck beneath my coat into my underwear. I walk silently, liking the sound of my shoes on the pavement. One step. Another. One step. Another. Though it only lasted a few days, the reminder of being close, but not quite there yet, is painful. Interesting, deliberating, funny, stimulating: these days shape a little part of me and how I will move forward.

I arrive at my flat and open the door. I drop my keys on the little ledge next to my door and slowly take off my shoes, coat, clothes. I pick up the mundane bits around the floor. I wash my face, not looking at it, wiping the first layer of makeup off with some tonic and the next layer with some scrub. I squeeze out the last of the cream tube and after using, throw it into the bin. I brush my hair and walk, naked, to the washing machine to get my dry laundered pyjamas out. I catch myself in the hallway mirror. I walk up to the thick brimmed frame and put my hand on the glass over my breast. I let it run down my body, looking at the reflection of lights from outside play on my hips. Eyes glassy, I smile.

Chapter Twenty

I sometimes watch, half in awe, half mocking, others flailing, pouring their energy into activities, that seem trivial or useless to me. Organised group activities in which individuals delegate one another to sing, dance or participate in some form of cultural busyness. Occasionally, depending on the degree of talent, I admire the courage or the discipline involved in preparing and training a certain stirring of happening. Most times, if it is not linked to some form of expertise- but simply a form of time consumption or socialising agent, I mock. For some reason, in those moments, I become cruel and feel that I am somehow higher in understanding; understanding what needs to be done to move forward and what can be left undone. My best friend at high school, a bustling soul, full of kindness, spent hours doing all those extra things that get stuffed into your day with some thought, but with little actual purpose. She would call it a great skill of mine to prioritise. Others said I was missing out on the fabric of life; that this is what we live for. The journeys and processes of coming together are what meshes lives. Any form of interaction is another experience and another story that you meet.

A fear of not having lived properly overcomes me sometimes. Suddenly and out of the blue it will rip over my body in an unexpected wave, disrupting an organised acceptance and almost placid appreciation of the past. I have had opportunities that some people would not be able to conjure in their wildest dreams and yet I stuck so close to the path of necessity. I did not, as they say, live life to the fullest. Accompanied by my family and books, I have lived happily and safely. But I have not gone to a wild campus college in the mountains or at the beach. I have not learnt Japanese or piano or hockey. I have not embraced the beauty of my youth with a confidence that blows minds. I have not experienced true romantic, passionate, earth-shocking love. I have not lived freely, in a way that would let me enjoy the pleasure of the luxurious easiness that I was born into. Instead, I calculated the quickest, fastest path of necessity. I skipped the superfluous. And in those moments of sudden fear, I realise this. And although I am still in the first quarter of my life I fear it is too late because I know the person that I am and I fear that that will never change.

*

I am due to see Zafira around 12 a.m. for coffee. I don't quite know what to expect and how to prepare for whatever awaits me. She texted me last night and we had arranged to meet at Pimlico Fresh and I thought we could walk over to Battersea Park for a little stroll. The sun is shining brightly and the lightly coloured sky is wide and open. Taking care not to reveal too much skin, I dress in a pair of jeans and a deep red turtleneck jumper. I quickly spot her standing outside, her head covered with soft grey material.

"Zafira!" I call.

"Clara! Hello!" She smiles at me and her eyes shine beautifully.

"It's so lovely to see you," I say. "I'm glad it worked out."

"Me too. Thank you so much for taking the time," she replies. "I'm sure you're a busy woman." She looks at me almost hopefully.

"Oh! Don't fool yourself. I'm less busy than I would like to be."

We grab two mint teas plus a big slice of banana bread to share and walk towards the park. I'm a little nervous. Maybe it's because of the circumstances in which Zafira and I first met. Wishing to break the silence, I gesture towards the bread we are both picking at and ask: "Is it true we share 50% of our DNA with bananas?"

"Not exactly," she laughs. "That statistic is a little misleading, but it does reflect quite accurately the fact that most human genes have some sort of parallel or equivalent in other organisms. Even the humble banana."

"If humans are so similar to other organisms, how can it be that we are so profoundly different? Can it really be a matter of just a few genes?"

"Well…" She pauses, gathering her thoughts. "When scientists first started studying DNA, it took them a long time to figure out what a gene actually is. Eventually, a picture began to emerge, which seemed to demonstrate that roughly 3% of DNA constituted what we think of as 'genes', while the vast majority, 97%, was considered junk."

"Junk?" I ask, incredulously.

"Essentially. Think of it this way. If I gave you an alphabet of just three letters, you could organise them in a variety of ways, randomly or deliberately, and sometimes you would end up with a recognisable word. But most of the time you would end up with nonsense. In other words: 'junk'. This idea can be applied to the formation of proteins in genes. A gene has a very special organisation and sequence of nucleotides, which can be turned into a protein, and if the sequence is wrong it doesn't make a useful protein. So, for DNA to make proteins it requires grammar. It's a molecular language. A lot of it doesn't make sense, but the bits that do? They're what we call genes."

"So, what's the junk for, then?"

"A lot of the junk is actually what we call 'Control Mechanisms'. It's like driving a car: you can't just drive straight the entire time, but need to adjust to twists and turns, changes in the quality of the road, traffic, and where your ultimate destination is. So, a lot of what is, or was, thought to be junk, may not contain instructions for genes, but it does contain instructions for these control elements."

"But they can't control every aspect of our nature, can they? What impact does that have on our understanding of nurture?"

"Well, that's where epigenetics comes into the equation. Epigenetics is the idea that your life can change how you express your genes. If DNA is a language, then think of your life as a book. Just as a book is more likely to fall open at a particular page, because of the way it is bound or because the spine is bent from the reader returning again and again to their favourite chapter, your life is more likely to lead in a certain direction because of certain formative influences. So, the fact that your parents cared for you, might make it so that the book is more likely to fall open on page 124 than page 324."

"But that would mean that everything about us is determined by, or can be explained by, our genes," I respond. doubtfully. "That seems far too...cold."

"You really think so?" She asks. "I find it quite beautiful. Let's stick with the analogy I've already been using. Imagine a library, to which everyone has access. Any one of us is capable of reading any and every book in the library, but none of us will do so in exactly the same order or in exactly the same conditions. So, the order in which you read can determine whether you become interested in literature, or engineering, or simply become someone who hates reading. In much the same way, we all have the same genes and the same genetic potential, but people turn out differently because they've read different books at different times, so to speak, or had different librarians guiding them through the shelves."

"So, if I'd read the same books in the same order as Usain Bolt, or had the same librarians he had, then I'd be able to run as fast as him?"

"No. You might be more likely to be able to run at such speeds, but no two people can ever turn out exactly the same, no matter how similar their circumstances may be."

"I thought you just said that we all have the same genetic library!"

"Yes, but none of us enter that library through the same door. In order to run as fast as Usain Bolt, not only would you have to read the same books in the same order, but your parents would need to have matched his parents, book for book. Same with your grandparents, and so on. Moreover, if a gene is like a book, not every copy of that book will be identical. You might have the same book in different editions, or languages. You and Usain Bolt may both have the same book, the Bible for example, but he can have the King James Version and you might have a copy in Cantonese, or Swahili, or Braille. These differences help explain why, given how remarkably similar the DNA of any two people may be, they can still be so remarkably dissimilar."

My mind is whirring as our conversation comes to a natural lull. Eventually, remembering her presence, I ask:

"What does your name mean, Zafira? It sounds so beautiful. Za-fi-ra." I pronounce each syllable with care, like she once did with mine.

"It means 'victorious' or – she searches for a meaning in our language – successful."

"Well that's quite apt. Your knowledge…the way you express yourself: that is what I would call success." I look at her in admiration.

"If only I could use it. I don't feel successful at all. I have all this knowledge and can't do anything with it."

"You haven't explained why exactly."

Zafira looks away with a torn expression on her face. "I can't, Clara. You forget, I am married to a man who is very powerful and has a very clear idea of what a woman should do. The fact that I could study was amazing in itself. I received a scholarship and had to persuade him for months. Eventually he conceded, under the condition that I still stood by and was, of course, available to him whenever he needed me."

"What about the other women?"

"Yes, we are three wives. I am the only one that studied. A matchmaker made the match."

"Are you in love with him?" I daringly ask the obvious question.

"I don't think I know what love is," she responds, tentatively.

"I don't either," I say, and touch her hand in solidarity.

"But you can find out one day."

"I hope that I will. But – I try to be careful in choosing my words – do you not love Ahmad at all?"

She responds quickly: "How can I love a man who denies me the right to work, to research the things that I am passionate about?"

"What is he scared of?"

"I honestly don't know. I don't understand if it's his ego or if it's just because it would be a break in his family's tradition. But I have tried to persuade him for so long and he does not understand my motivation to work. He does not understand that I think this is the most relevant and exciting thing for me to be doing right now."

"I don't know what to say. I wish that I could help you, Zafira, but I am also wary of getting involved." She visibly shudders at my words.

"No! Definitely no involvement."

"See, that's what I thought. I feel a little as though I am treading on eggshells. I don't want to generalise or seem patronising."

"You aren't patronising, you don't have to worry about that."

"That's what you think, but I have been in so many situations in which I want to understand and help people in a less fortunate position than my own and they react angrily towards the way I phrase things. I used to take a module at university on race and empire. Everyone in the class was black, except for me. Anything I said could be construed as some form of ignorance. We were discussing the terrors of colonialism and white superiority. And there I was: white and privileged. The product of the British Empire, whose successes are built on past exploitation. I embodied, and often feel that I still do embody, the superficial characteristics of what they were fighting against. And so, they didn't really let me show myself beyond the exterior. I don't blame them, but it's made me wary of expressing criticism towards other cultures."

"Listen, I get where you're coming from, but this is pretty straightforward. I'm not bashing my whole culture. I'm angry at my husband, who is stuck in old traditions. Traditions which, by the way, also existed in Europe.

Women haven't been allowed to work in almost every country at some point in time. And I hate it."

"Couldn't you work for him? I heard that he is heavily invested in his own genetic research fund." I weakly attempt to think of anything, knowing that whatever I say will have already been on her mind.

"It's not his fund. He's a large shareholder, but I don't want to work for them. Even if I could."

"What do you mean?"

"They specialise in genetic alteration. And don't get me wrong, I'm aware that a lot of good can be done through genetically engineering what we have been given by God, but it is so dangerous if in the wrong hands."

"Is it in the wrong hands?"

"I don't know the other shareholders personally, but if they're anything like Ahmad then, yes. These are people with buckets of money looking to engineer efficiency as an investment."

As she says this, my heart plummets and I suddenly realise that I nudged the money that Arthur is making back into Ahmad's hands, through my involvement. I feel faint and hold onto the riverside wall, looking down at my reflection. Wavy and disfigured. I look away.

"Are you alright?" Zafira asks.

"I'm fine." I push my nausea back inside, away from the present. "What would happen if you just did it, if you just went and saw my friend Hugo for an interview?"

Her eyes darken and she looks down at the ground. "If I did that and Ahmad found out, he...he would...Look...I can't." Zafira stutters and starts nervously adjusting her headdress. "I have to leave now, Clara. It was so nice to be able to talk. I rarely get to share this stuff."

"Zafira, what does he do to you?" I ignore her attempt to wave it off, and have to refrain myself from turning her around so that she can look me in the eye.

"You wouldn't understand. It's not as bad as it seems."

"What is it?"

"He gets a little aggressive, that's all. It's okay. I'm fine."

"How aggressive?"

"I don't know how to explain it. He just grabs me and...It's more the way he looks at me whilst..."

"Zafira, this is not okay. Whatever the culture, whatever the tradition he is holding onto, this is your physical safety. This is your life! You have to find a way to get out of this."

"I told you, you wouldn't understand! I can't get out. This is it! We don't do divorce, if that's what you're thinking of. Our families are involved. I would disgrace mine. I...I can't."

"Zafira..."

"No. Enough. I don't want to talk about this anymore."

"But..."

"No. I have to leave anyway. Maybe I'll see you again. Will you be at Ahmad's exhibition?"

"Yes."

"Goodbye."

"Bye Zafira. Take care of yourself."

As I look at her striding towards the park exit, I can't help but quietly repeat her words out loud: *Ahmad's Exhibition. Arthur's Exhibition? Ahmad's Exhibition. Arthur's Exhibition? Ahmad. Arthur.*

Ahmad and Arthur.

I decide to call Arthur.

"Hello?"

"Listen…I just met with Zafira, you know, one of Ahmad's wives…"

"What? Why would you do that? Clara, come on, what's going on?"

"You can't give him the money. You shouldn't even be giving him the sculptures. Arthur, I'm serious."

"Clara, that's enough. We've already been through this."

"No, please hear me out. He's still aggressive to his wives, and to God knows who else."

"Clara…"

"And this genetic fund he mentioned? That's not where you want your money to go. He isn't the type of guy we want making decisions about how our genes are engineered! And…"

"Clara. Stop. It's too late. He was here this morning with the revised contract. I signed it."

"What?"

"The sculptures are being picked up later this week."

"But…"

"Let it go."

"I can't."

"You have to. It's done. I have to go, I'm meeting a client in a moment. I'll see you soon."

"But…Okay…I…Goodbye then."

"Goodbye Clara."

Chapter Twenty-one

It is about a month later, and I've seen neither Arthur nor Zafira since. I'm sitting in an Uber on my way to the gallery, holding the thickly printed invitation to the opening of the exhibition in my hands. Red block letters spell out: *MODERN WOMEN. ARTHUR ADLER x AHMAD HASSAN*. The car whizzes past little individual shops and businesses and I begin to imagine how at some point they will all be replaced by online merchants. My mind spirals into suddenly gripping fears of a future in which AI and technology rule a world that is already losing its romance. In which screens, on screens, dictate our lives.

The car slows and I'm pulled out of my abstracted reverie. I am wearing a deep navy floor-length tunic dress. My arms are weighed down by layers of long, billowing flared sleeves and my blonde head is covered with the same matching deep blue, silk fabric. I step out of the car and into the courtyard that opens into the gallery. Packed with people, I push through the crowd making my way to the entrance. Large red flags with the title '*MODERN WOMEN. ARTHUR ADLER x AHMAD HASSAN*' hang from the exterior walls, fluttering in the wind. A flurry of people walks past me. All of which are Arab men in dark suits. Some are wearing their traditional white gowns, but not many. I very quickly spot Arthur standing at the far end of the entrance hall, flocking from one person to the next. Oozing confidence and grandeur, he answers questions earnestly, smiling flippantly at eager onlookers. His hair is held back behind his ears with some sort of gel. In place of his usual linen shirt and trouser look, is a crisp white shirt under a very loose, almost old-fashioned look-ing blue suit. I stare at him a little too long and he catches my eye from across the room.

Momentary confusion at my appearance is quickly re-placed by recognition and a questioning raised eyebrow. The strength that I had built up before my arrival falters and I melt a little at the sight of him. Surrounded by press and admirers I realise the importance of this event to his career and, from the look on his face, I know that doing this was never a question for him, that doing this was al-ways very clear for him. I pick up my hand and, cocking my head a little, lightly wave towards him. He waves back, gesturing for me to come over when somebody taps his shoulder and the moment is gone.

Arthur turns towards the new arrival and I begin to make my way forward, relishing the fact that I am almost unrecognisable in my dress. It's difficult to describe, but I feel beautifully concealed and mysteriously sensual. If someone does look my way, they look at my face and we talk, or rather tease with our eyes. I show my invitation and step into the exhibition rooms. The space is filled with men, frolicking around female sculptures. About 60% of the guests look Middle Eastern, of which maybe 10% are women. The remaining roughly 40% of interna-tional guests are relatively equally divided in terms of gender. A young Italian woman walks past me, talking loudly to her girlfriend. Both are wearing tight low-cut dresses.

My eyes wander towards the artwork. The women that I know. The clay that I have touched and felt with my own hands. The curved breasts, plump buttocks, bulging or firm bellies and dainty arms fill the room. Every corner is decorated with another. I skim the room, in awe of the talent. Walking between the masses of canapé-eating and champagne-slurping people, I focus on the clay. Body upon body. I quickly realise that I am looking for my own body. Searching eyes bore out of my face, studying each figure that I am faced with. One more. Another. The next. I walk quickly, tracing the circular path curated to navigate the art. Back at the door, I am overcome with a feeling of emptiness. Nothing. No impact. No purpose. What is all this? Why am I here? I see a young man touching a sculpture, grazing his hand down a female back and I feel a surge of anger.

"Are you alright, Miss?" A volunteer wearing a name-tag labelled 'Tom' looks at me.

"...Is this alright? Are they allowed to be touching the artwork?"

"Yes," he chuckles. "The creative minds behind all this," he gestures into the room, "are attempting to break the barrier between the expectations and reality of female bodies."

"I see."

"Are you enjoying the exhibition?"

"I...I suppose so."

"Do you have any questions or something you would like me to elaborate on?" He smiles kindly.

"I...Has Arthur...I mean, do you think that the artist has made some sort of statement in his work?"

"Interesting question. He is definitely alluding to a number of sociological and gendered themes, regarding the pressures that women face today, what with social media..."

I ignore most of what he goes on to say, letting his pre-prepared patter slide past me.

"...Have you got a favourite piece?" Tom looks at me with large eyes.

"Um…I'm not sure…I probably find the curled-up woman over there the most interesting." I point towards the wooden knot that I had touched in Arthur's studio. Looking at it now, I admire its curled-up position. "What about you? Do you have a favourite?"

"Ah. Yes, I do. Definitely. Have you had a chance to look at 'Clara'?"

My heart jolts. "Excuse me?"

"The 'Clara' piece? It's over there in the annex."

"The annex." I say more to myself than to Tom.

"Yes, the small room that people are lining up in front of over there. Would you like to have a look at it?" I nod wordlessly, unable to speak and Tom starts walking towards the line of only about five people. There is a white opening in the wall. Easy to miss, if you don't look closely. A man standing by the doorway lets two people in, as two walk out.

"Adler asked for it to only be viewed in pairs of strangers. We don't know why, but you are not allowed to go in alone and you are not allowed to go in with somebody you know.".

"Only pairs of strangers," I repeat quietly.

"Yes, precisely." Tom looks at me, a little perplexed, and we stand waiting in silence, as the line gently shuffles forward. I suddenly feel hot and the fabric around my head and neck tightens. I shift it around and start breathing laboriously. As I get closer to the door, two people walking out of the room brush up against me from both sides and I begin to feel claustrophobic. I feel my face redden and hands dampen and begin to aggressively pull off the silk covering my head. The two Italian women walk by again and I am suddenly overcome with the desire to rip off my whole tunic and feel air float around my legs and arms and through my hair and around my neck. Tom stares at me, with a questioning look on his face.

"Are you sure that you are."

"Yes. I'm fine."

It is our turn and we walk into the room. White walls and white floors and a white ceiling give way to my figure. The reddish clay shapes my body up until my neck, at which a sharp cut has removed my head. I gravitate towards the sculpture, eyes welling up and confused. I reach out to touch the headless thing when Tom exclaims, "Excuse me! It is forbidden to touch this sculpture."

"But…I don't understand. I thought you said…" and as I speak, I look at a large plaque on the stand that reads PLEASE DO NOT TOUCH. I take a step back, leaning against the wall and stare at the figure that so closely resembles my own, yet which I cannot touch.

"What do you know about this piece?" I ask in a whisper.

"Very little to be honest. This is the only sculpture in the exhibition that does not have a head. It is clear that this was done after the sculpture had originally been completed. You can see the ridges and edges that once bordered onto something…"

Arthur steps into the room and finishes Tom's sentence "– something…someone who was always thinking. More often than not, it was probably overthinking. What would you say, Clara?" Tom's eyes widen as my name sinks in and, without either of us noticing, he discretely leaves the room.

"Arthur," I whisper.

"Hi Clara."

"You're not a stranger," I state.

"I know. But almost…I haven't seen you in a while…"

"Yes, that's true."

"And that's okay." He smiles. "I'm glad you found your way to this part of the exhibition."

"What is this part of the exhibition?"

"I don't really know." He walks towards me. "What I do know, is that you didn't want me to do this." He laughs a little. "Now, I can't say I'm sure what it is you do want, but I wasn't going to put your head in this exhibition knowing that it wasn't what you wanted."

"But what about my body?"

"Well…I thought this way it might be a bit of a symbol; an act of defiance. A mind that wasn't in agreement. A body that had to stay, effectively becoming an object. You know Edison once said that 'The chief function of the body is to carry the brain around'. Without your head, this isn't you, Clara. It's just a bit of clay that could resemble any female on earth."

"That's true. And yet you still named her Clara."

"I did. I hope you're okay with that."

"I am," I say, and I realise as I say it that it's true. I am actually okay with some part of myself being represented here.

"Why pairs of strangers?"

"Sometimes all you need is to step out of what you know…another opinion really…to understand that nothing in this world is fixed or true. We all make our own reality."

In a way, my entanglement with Arthur was much like a pair of strangers walking into an unknown space, just like this little cubicle. It is so easy to get lost in the world we are presented with. And even easier to get stuck in a version of this world, surrounded by like-minded individuals who all tread the same path. Arthur and I disagreed and such disagreements are enough to show us that everything that we do or think is exactly that: something that *we* do or *we* think. There are endless ways to live this life. There are infinite versions of what is said to be known or true or real. These bodies, these women surrounding me in all their different forms, are individuals who do not need to be called fabulous or beautiful, because they just are what they are. I am what I am. I am what I think. I think there is a lot to learn. And I think there is a lot to live for.

I walk out of the room, leaving Arthur with a flutter of admirers. I walk out of the gallery, awash with a sense of urgency to explore the world, its people, its cultures. To make my own reality.

As I step out of the door, I see Hassan's wives in one corner of the foyer. I search for Zafira, but cannot find her eyes in the midst of their layers of fabric. I walk over.

"Hello ladies. Is Zafira here?"

"No, I am sorry…she isn't here."

"Where is she?" I ask.

"We don't know. She left us a week ago."

Chapter Twenty-two

I want

to be able to stand firmly
rooted in myself, letting things
come and go.
Conversely, I want to float,
letting myself grow.

I want to study art,
Shapes, colours, form and figures.
Let their history
seep into me.

I want to drink prose and
poetry- to learn from
chronicled passion
and pain.

I want to stand in a
wild field alone;
or on a windy mountain;
or between quick white rimmed waves

and feel everything.

And still be free;
to be able to
view it all
from a distance
like Lord Henry says:

as though watching a movie.

To let myself grow and deepen
through experience
and novelty
and longing

but to always
stay rooted
in a peace of mind-
the knowledge that
I
myself
am the vessel of
a wondrous concoction of
experience
and emotion
and that what we call
life.

And that
I
myself
will be at peace
with colours, books,
poetry, fields,
the ocean, the moon.

Thank you to my two incredible parents and five siblings, Max, Josephine, Felix, Julinka, Pablo, for a lifetime of love and encouragement.

To my high school English teacher, mentor and editor, Dr Eamon Byers, my deepest thanks for your constant support, motivation and feedback.

For reading and commenting on the manuscript, I thank both my parents Karl-Georg and Christiane Altenburg, my sister Josephine, my aunts Diana von der Goltz and Catharina d'Aprile, my wonderful friends: Alexis Broschek (multiple readings!), Alick Salomon, Hugo Engel, Flora Camps-Harris, Hannah Inkster, Gloria and Grace Steinmark.

For letting me pick your brains on genetics, evolution and game theory, I thank Andre Fenton, Kuljinder Chase and Tariq Enver.

Table of contents